CANOPLES INVESTIGATIONS
TACKLES SPACE PIRATES

KC SPRAYBERRY

Freaky Fiction Writing * Spring

Freaky Fiction Writing is located on the web:

Facebook:

  http://facebook.com/ffw2013

Blog:

  http://freakyfictionwriting.wordpress.com

Twitter:

  http://twitter.com/FreakyWriting

Table of Contents

CHAPTER ONE 1

CHAPTER TWO 12

CHAPTER THREE 21

CHAPTER FOUR 29

CHAPTER FIVE 37

CHAPTER SIX 43

CHAPTER SEVEN 51

CHAPTER EIGHT 58

CHAPTER NINE 66

CHAPTER TEN 73

CHAPTER ELEVEN 80

CHAPTER TWELVE 88

CHAPTER THIRTEEN 94

CHAPTER FOURTEEN 102

CHAPTER FIFTEEN 108

CHAPTER SIXTEEN 116

CHAPTER SEVENTEEN 124

CHAPTER EIGHTEEN 133

CHAPTER NINETEEN 140

CHAPTER TWENTY 147

CHAPTER TWENTY-ONE 154

CHAPTER TWENTY-TWO 163

CHAPTER TWENTY-THREE 168

CHAPTER TWENTY-FOUR   176

CHAPTER TWENTY-FIVE   183

CHAPTER TWENTY-SIX   189

CHAPTER TWENTY-SEVEN   195

CHAPTER TWENTY-EIGHT   204

CHAPTER TWENTY-NINE   211

ABOUT THE AUTHOR   218

CHAPTER ONE

My life changed on an impossibly ordinary day. No warnings came my way, nothing to indicate that all I believe in is about to change -- for the worst.

As I think back on it after all the space dust settles, I wish someone had given me a warning. I was about to embark on the biggest adventure of my life. Nothing would make me change a second of that very exciting day.

Nothing marks this Thursday as extraordinary. Canoples Station orbits Jupiter, and my eyes pop open like they do every other day. The illumination in my quarters changes from artificial moonlight to artificial sunlight at the same time it does every other day. My mom and older brother get ready for work like they always do. Even I get into the act by zapping breakfast while they take their sonic showers. When I, BD Bradford, take over a kitchen, watch out galaxy. Great teen food is about to erupt.

"What are your plans for today?" Mom pushes the pancakes around her plate.

They look more like asteroids after impact than pancakes. Lesson learned. Zapping everyone's breakfast at the same time is a rotten idea.

Wade, my nauseatingly perfect older brother, eats the food without commenting. Kind of makes me feel worthless, as usual, but only worthless cooking. Nothing else in my life is lousy.

Uh, well, that's not quite true. But that problem I have to solve at another time, as soon as I figure out girls.

"Nothing," I tell Mom around a mouthful of the mashed pancakes. "Hang around the promenade. Look up Carl and Terry. You know. Same old thing."

She and Wade glance at each other, exchanging a look I know all too well. *Gotta work on my "I'm not up to anything face."* They can't ruin one of my last days of freedom with made up chores to keep me out of trouble.

Where is it? Come on, don't disappoint me. One of you gives me that unwanted advice you hand out every other day.

Mom opens her mouth but snaps her lips together when a vu-screen on the refrigerator flickers on. My heart pounds in anticipation of the upcoming broadcast. Sweat beads my forehead.

Saved by the governor's idea of an important announcement. Someone in the Milky Way loves me!

"Attention residents of Canoples Station." To the accompaniment of the disembodied computer voice, a visual of the Twelve Stations logo fills the vu-screen. "Several space-liner captains have reported encounters with possible space pirates during the station's sleep cycle. All small flitters are advised to remain on the station. Tour shuttles may launch, but at their own risk. Larger ships should check with

Security before departing the station. That is all."

That is all? Who thinks up these messages?

Questions zoom through my head – what do the space pirates look like? How many are there? What kind of ships do they fly?

My mind whirls with ways to get off the station so my buds and I can track down the space pirates. Bringing in those criminals will keep us in creds for a week or two.

"I know that look." Mom's flat tone of voice brings me back to reality. "You won't get involved, BD. Or else."

Cold fear cramps my muscles. I see the color red, as in red chips spelling my doom. Those are Mom's way of telling me that I've gone too far. If I get five or more in a week, my whole life swirls into a black hole.

"Me? Get involved?" My voice squeaks, and I swallow a couple of times. "Would I break the rules?"

She and Wade cover their mouths and cough. They sound more like a couple of laughing Pluto baboons.

"Stay out of trouble, BD." Wade stands and dusts food bits off his pukey green jumpsuit. His uniform is the most awful color I have ever seen; a greenish-yellow that resembles what I did after eating a bad Gut-Buster pizza. "See you tonight, Mom. Chief Pelham probably needs everyone on duty to deal with this problem," Wade says.

He stares at me for six extremely long heartbeats.

"Don't dig up any new "cases." Leave anything you see that's wrong to Security."

There it is. No matter how rushed he is, Wade always finds a way to mention me staying out of trouble. He always makes my life as miserable as he can, but I refuse to let him stop me today.

After he leaves, I spend a couple of minutes checking out files from my business, one Wade keeps trying to shut down despite how successful it is. Mom attacks the breakfast mess in the kitchen. No matter how rushed she is, she never breaks her own rule. The person who makes the meal skates on cleaning duty, which is why I zapped those pancakes on the highest setting and in half the recommended time.

"Later, Mom," I call after shoving my PerSys to one side. "Gotta catch up with Terry and Carl."

She pokes her head out of the kitchen. I race for the door in an attempt to avoid whatever she has on her mind.

What did I do now? Why is she tracking me like I'm still three?

"Do something with your hair," she says. "I don't mind it long, but I won't let you run around with it a mess."

Rats!

My hair is an argument whenever she and Wade think I'm acting up. Unlike most of the station residents, mine comes down to my shoulders, and it has a whole lot of waves in it. Usually, I run a comb through it, and forget about it. Her order means I have to bind my hair back, so if she happens to see (me) sometime today, she'll have proof that I didn't ignore her.

Frustrated by her speed, I sprint into the refresher and yank a comb through my unruly, wavy, shoulder length black hair. As I fasten a clip at neck level, deep black eyes peer back at me from the mirror and what looks like a zit raises a bump on the tip of my nose. It doesn't matter that I'm seventeen, those pesky teen abominations still appear at the worst moments. Thankfully, in the twenty-fourth century, all we need to do is apply a bit of patch powder to the offensive bump before it grows to the point where everyone will notice, which I do with all due speed. Then, with nervous energy charging my wiry body, I sneak past the kitchen.

I make it to the corridor before she has a change of heart, and figures I need to hang around our quarters all day cleaning or moving stuff around in a new decorating scheme she saw on the vid.

Thoughts run through my head, absolutely ordinary thoughts. The same kind of thoughts I have every other day. This is nothing more than an ordinary day, one with the promise of hanging around the promenade, gaming with my buds, and longing for my gal to talk to me. No thoughts of doing serious work enter my mind. School is a far off threat – when I have to return on Monday. This is my last semester break as a kid, and I plan to enjoy every second. By this time next year, I will have celebrated my eighteenth birthday and be on my way to the Law Enforcement Academy on Mars. Like most other kids on the station, I'm following in my family's footsteps in my career choice, but there are other options I still want to explore.

Life on a space station just can't get any better than it is this fine morning. The best part is figuring out a way to take on those space pirates. Maybe not today, but I'll find those creeps before school drags me back into homework and tests Monday morning!

I saunter toward the stairs just beyond the lifts with nothing more important on my mind than when Canoples Investigations will get another job to replace the creds I spent last week. The newest version of Asteroids debuts today. My plans include acing the fantastic game involving a masterful demonstration of flying skills to destroy an asteroid shower before it trashes any of the Twelve Stations. Then I can sit back and teach those without my enviable skills how to survive the massive meteor storm at the end – the hook ad I've seen for the last two months during the advertising blitz.

"Gotta figure out how to convince Carl and Terry to hunt down those space pirates." I nod. "We'll show Security how to keep the station safe from marauders."

I reach for the door, but at the last second, my hand freezes. Now, I'm not one of those fools who believe in premonitions or anything else so dumb. I have this ugly feeling running through my body, and I never ignore ugly feelings. Eyes darting in all directions, I step away from the door before someone catches me breaking a rule.

"BD."

Mom's voice brings a terror I barely manage to hide. Only two people have the power to do what she has, and the other stopped speaking to me a while back after we had a fight. I turn around and gulp at the look on her face, a mixture of flat out fury and exasperation.

"Your computers are all over the place." She reaches past me to push the lift actuator. "Clean up before you find your friends."

"We have a job," I respond, hoping she believes me.

She has this funny talent that lets her spot lies on the other side of the galaxy, but only if the other person looks away from her. With one glaring exception. Me. Not that I keep a scorecard or anything, but I can count on the fingers of one hand how many times I got away with lying to her, and have a couple of those fingers left over.

Besides, I can't look her in the eye and lie. Impossible. To stare into those hazel eyes, still holding a hint of grief over my dad's death seven years ago, and even think about trying to fool her puts a nasty feeling in my stomach that has nothing to do with my love for Gut-Buster Pizzas. My eyes focus on a bulkhead behind her right ear, and I work hard on not shifting my feet around on the deck.

"The job can wait," Mom says.

A ding takes her attention away from my face. *Thank you, whoever made sure the lift arrived!* She reads me better than the vid-romances she loves. The lift doors open, and she goes inside.

"Remember, clean up your mess *before* you find your friends." Mom holds up a finger.

Hoo, boy, I sure don't want to see that ever again.

One single finger is all it takes to put cold fear into my body. Fear I work very hard to shove into the deep recesses of my mind. What she wants me to do will take all of two seconds. Who am I to ignore her simple request?

7

Unless you live inside a glass station without any connection to the rest of the galaxy, I'm BD Bradford, intrepid investigator. Nothing scares me. Nothing at all. Except my mom holding up one finger after telling me to do something. But I can't take those lousy two seconds to do what she wants. Later, much later will work, long before she comes home. Now, I have of a very important mission, one that won't wait.

Our gazes lock, and I hope Mom understands I'll do what she wants, but when I have time, not on her schedule. After another ding, the lift doors close, and she disappears from sight, to spend the day working in the pediatric section of the station's hospital. Mom is a nurse, a good one, and often comes home wiped from everything she has to do. Kids, according to her, never change no matter how many rules adults put on them. If she bothers to ask, I can explain. All kids love trying the impossible, even if it hurts them. A great example lives with her; I never slow down when facing danger.

My immediate problem lies back in my quarters, and I have no desire to waste time cleaning up a couple of computers I'll put back where I left them later.

"Sorry, Mom." I walk over to the door leading to the stairs and open it. "No way will I let anyone get the drop on me playing Asteroids."

Using the stairs burns off some of the nervous energy I've felt all morning. I'm not sure why, but I have the feeling me and my buds are about to dive into the biggest case of our career and need to be where the action happens. On Canoples Station, that's either Io, one of

Jupiter's moons, or the promenade. Since I have no reason to join the scientists studying the volcano about to erupt, there is only one other place – the teen gathering zone. I take the stairs two at a time and arrive on the promenade in seconds. Even though it's only eight, teens already surround the shops and arcades.

The sounds and smells, so familiar to a boy raised on one of the Twelve Stations, invite me to join the fun. But I'm no ordinary boy. No one living on the Twelve Stations classifies themselves as ordinary. All of us descend from Earth's survivors, after humans abandoned the dying planet during the mid-twenty-first century. Global warming caused weird storms, and left residents fighting to survive. Every government got together and decided to evacuate to stations built as part of the United States exploration of the Milky Way. No ships ever went back to the planet. If someone wants to, they can view the massive storms and pollution still hanging around after three centuries when they visit Aldebbaran Station. No urge ever prods me to ask Mom to go there. Like most teens, visiting a planet filled with a bunch of politicians sounds boring.

"Where are they?" I search for my buds, but they're nowhere in sight.

It's early. Maybe Carl Wills and Terry Ashley decided to catch a few more zzzs before showing up to join the fun.

I take off across the promenade with determination in my step. Gaming Zone is clear on the other side. Unless I ignore everyone and everything around me, the chances of making it to my destination before one of my many friends, or enemies, stops me are zero.

My quarry in sight, I freeze in shocked amazement when the emergency klaxon blares. Glances to the left and right provides no insight as to what troubles the station. Asking one of the Security types now racing for the lifts and stairs will do no good. None of them like me much, except the chief and my older brother. They tolerate me because I come up with solutions to problems, and show them how I figured it out. Wade says I shove my solutions into everybody's face, but he's my brother. What does he know?

Left to figure out what's going on myself, a situation I love, I begin a slow check of the stores and arcades. There's nothing unusual going on, but a bunch of people hanging at the doors stare at something behind me. That leaves one choice. I spin around, and my mouth drops open.

Five flitters arrow around the massive tetra-flex porthole giving everyone a view of Jupiter and her moons. These are ships capable of seating two to four people for station-to-planet hops. The largest thing in sight, Io, is in synchronous orbit between the station and Jupiter. According to a science team on the moon's surface, its volcano might erupt soon. More than anything, I hope they figure out if it really will happen soon. One of my best buds, Terry, wants his mom to come home. She's the lead scientist and has to stay until they complete their research.

Another worry settles around me as I stare at those flitters. From the maneuvers, it's obvious the pilots aren't a bunch of teens with a brand new license. They aim straight at the tetra-flex but veer off before striking it. Each ship is a different color with wild patterns, and what looks like strange animal faces painted on their forward area.

My immediate thought is pirates, but that's close to impossible. Pirates lie in wait along the space lanes between the stations and planets. They rob passengers of long distance liners and avoid capture by roving Security patrols. My dad and his team vanished without a trace seven years ago while looking for a pirate gang harassing ships coming to Canoples. I long ago came to terms with losing him. Seeing evidence of the men who might have killed Dad starts a slow burn inside me, and a determination to figure out why pirates are attacking the station.

"The announcement," I whisper. "The pirates are real. There really are pirates at Canoples Station."

"Oh!" a girl squeals, turning my joyous thoughts into ones of disgust. "Those nasty pirates will steal us away. We'll never see our parents again!"

It's time for me to beat feet before I make the situation worse. The speaker is none other than the governor's daughter, and one of my sworn enemies. Deciding to check out the Canoples Investigations office for any jobs that might have come up, I race into the nearest stairwell and slide along the railing between floors. No way will Lisa Tulane ruin my day.

CHAPTER TWO

Canoples Investigations, the business that keeps me and my buds in creds, is on level eight right next to Security. I waste a few seconds watching the frenetic activity inside there, as the officers shout at each other about what they saw on the promenade.

"They were *not* pirates," a weasel woman hollers. "Pirates never come near stations." She stabs a finger into a male officer's chest. "Never! Do you get what I'm saying?"

"Bu-bu-but–" The male officer waves his hands in arcs and weaves, as he imitates what the pirates did. "They aimed right at the porthole on the promenade."

"Good grief!" She growls and steps toward the guy, who backs off fast. "You sound like a bunch of kids. What? Are you channeling BD Bradford and his friends?"

That's just about the worst comparison I've ever heard. I never act like the guy now looking like he wants to sink through the deck.

Well, almost never. Only for Mom … and Cassie.

The officer backs away. Good move on his part. I feel like doing the same, even with tetra-flex between me and the female Security officer.

"Sure looked like pirates to me," another man yells. "You didn't see the ships, Marrow. No one does up cockpits like that except pirates!"

The woman officer, Gena Marrow, has a rep for being hard as exterior bolts. Her reasoning? Women Security officers are as rare as spacewalkers, so she has to be meaner and nastier than the guys. She turns a fierce glare on the officer who dared to contradict her. He backs away with his hands held in front of him.

"Do you want to be the one to tell Pelham that you saw pirates?" Marrow suggests. "Go right ahead, Skinks. Be my guest – after you make sure you really saw pirates. Or maybe you like Jupiter duty?"

"Yeah. Okay." Skinks drops his hands and sits behind the counter. "I'll pull up the vid from Station Control and prove we saw pirates."

There is no sign of Wade and Chief Pelham. I wonder where they are, and what they're doing.

"The Chief and Wade are probably at the hospital or Station Control," I mutter. "But no one thinks to ask me about the ships. Why should they? It's not like any of those jerks think about asking anyone on the promenade the identity of those pilots or exactly what we saw."

I still am not sure about those pilots identities. Oh, I can make a very good guess, and so can those Security officers, if they take the time to think about what they saw. None of them will, though. No one likes to think about pirates let alone talk about them.

"Ah, this isn't getting me anywhere." I walk past the tetra-flex door and key in the code to my office. "Let's see what jobs we have waiting."

Once I settle at my desk, I open a Per-Sys, a computer much like those on Earth but a lot faster. We measure our speed in tera-bytes and start at four hundred million for a slower-than-a-hop-to-Jupiter, no artificial intelligence machine. Seconds after I turn on the power, I stare in shock at an i-mail, our way of sending electronic mail on the station. The message's contents makes me groan. When will someone ask us to find something interesting, like a secret cache of vid-games?

Never comes to mind. Then again, we might stumble onto a case that will not only increase our fame but also give us enough creds to retire.

Maybe. Boy, I sure hope so.

Visions of enough creds to fill a room dance through my head.

There's always a bounty for pirates from the space liner companies, but Security can't claim it. Last I heard, it was close to four hundred thousand creds. I grin. Carl, Terry, and I can sure use that reward!

First things first, though. Catching a bunch of pirates won't happen in time to score my own copy of Asteroids.

"Great. Just freakin' great." I forward the i-mail to my buds, and let them know where to meet me. Then I reread the message to figure out the best place to start. "Hoppin' space rocks! Why did she leave her travel bag near a garbage chute?"

The end of the message holds my attention, in a disgusted way.

"Is she kidding? What universe does she come from?"

We live in the Milky Way, but not all the evacuees from Earth ended up on space stations. A couple of the ships had mutinies when their passengers discovered they had to live in an enclosed environment. The people developed communities on a planet that supports human life, but I never give those losers a second thought. Too much happens around Canoples to worry about someone who never bothers to keep up with current affairs.

It looks like one of them found me. Even worse, she's the wife of Rendall Station's governor. An anti-station freak and a politician's wife all rolled up into one person. This will be very, very ugly, but I want my own copy of Asteroids. Rumor has it the developers hid a special level at the end. The urge to unlock the door and discover what happens after the meteor storm pushes me to send a return i-mail accepting a case common sense tells me to run from as fast as possible.

"Too bad Dad never told me how to handle a situation like this." My reflection on the monitor reminds me of him, and all his advice.

People say I look a lot like him, but they are so wrong. My ebony black hair is darker than space outside the many portholes on Canoples Station, and my deep green eyes are nowhere close to Dad's light gray eyes. His hair is black, but not quite as black as mine. He did a decent job running Security, and everyone liked him, but he also had a temper nowhere near as fearsome as mine. When he yelled, criminals listened. Then again, the crooks might have listened because they had no other choice.

Laws are a lot different in the twenty-fourth century. For one thing, no one catches a break anymore, and I mean no one. Even little kids have to go through sensitivity training and anger management classes if they mess up, but not babies. Our governors and law councils aren't quite that bad, but rumor has it they're thinking about training babies from the day they're born to live quiet, obedient lives. Of course, none of those men and women has run into me on a bad day. Well, a couple have, but they must have forgotten my modus operandi – return the customer's property as fast as possible no matter what I have to do.

All this still comes nowhere close to solving my major problem. Once again, C.I. has a boring, go nowhere case.

"Why can't someone lose something interesting?" I complain.

My fervent and constant wish might happen about the time the sun goes nova. I kick back and read the message again.

"We didn't open C. I. to find missing travel bags." I come to my feet.

Canoples Investigations began not long after my dad disappeared. Three buds and I wanted to find missing persons at first. Without easy access to a flitter and no funds to buy one, we decided to look for missing property to save our creds, except we keep coming up with other stuff to buy, stuff necessary to surviving as a teen on a space station. Our best investigator, the only girl on the team, quit a few months back. My fault, but I will never admit it out loud.

Is business suffering? A little, but only because her departure leaves us with one computer expert. Will I apologize? Not only will the sun have to go nova, a new galaxy has to appear complete with livable planets before I ever apologize. Cassie quitting makes almost no difference. We go right on finding things people lose or tracking down computer problems except for one tiny detail. Creds now split three ways instead of four.

"Works for me." I stretch and walk out the door, making sure the lock engages. "But it sure would be nice if Cassie would speak to me once in a while."

If I time everything right, Terry and Carl arrive on the lift right as I reach it. Briefing them about our newest case while we make our way to the top of the station will save time.

The lift doors slide open, and I run the last couple of feet. Sure enough, there they are.

"How's it hanging?" Carl smirks. "Still trying to outgrow me?"

"I quit stretching exercises a year ago," I say.

To my dismay, when every other guy my age started shooting up, I remained a puny five-feet, four-inches, and endured a whole bunch of teasing about shrimp status. I tried every method listed on the local 'net to make myself grow, until nature accomplished what all those exercises, nasty tasting drinks, and lotions failed to produce. Almost overnight, I sprang up to a respectable six feet.

"Sure!" His smirk fades as I step into the lift.

Carl Wills, SpaceBall player, overall great guy, and our former female investigator's twin, tops me by a micrometer, but it's enough to get him into some things ahead of me. Stuff like flitter classes go by height not age. So, while I drool all over the porthole off the SpaceDock, he learns all the moves in one of the six-person shuttles, but he also teaches me on a sim whenever the instructor leaves.

I finally reached the right height and thanks to his assistance, have no problems acing the classes. But I still have another month before I can take the license exam for the third time. To my embarrassment, I can't achieve a manual landing without breaching one of the safety lasers. More time on a sim is in my future, like every night until the test next week.

Carl's uber-blonde hair hides the brown streaks giving Cassie's face a glow, and he is never one to ignore the latest trend. Right now, beach vids from the twentieth century are making the rounds in Galactic Multi-Plex. He gives his newest passion the full treatment by having his hair cut in a shaggy style and doing surf sims whenever he ditches us, or so he thinks. Terry and I have tons of pics we plan to post on our website. All the best ones are of Carl falling on his butt.

Sure looks dumb, standing on a thin board in a massive body of water called an ocean and riding on a wave. Anyone trying that now will find themselves sentenced to ten years of talking to the psych a hundred times a day and popping a bunch of happy candy. The docs always ignore me and my buds before they decide teens have no ability to think for themselves. We sure try to change their minds daily.

"That i-mail sounds super serious," Terry Ashley says. "Did you send a follow-up to find out why she thinks someone stole her bag?"

"Nah." I stare at the flashing numbers. "Why bother explaining? She's an anti-station freak and married to Rendall's governor. We don't have a century to make her understand."

"So great," he mumbles. "Not."

Terry stands as tall as Carl, making both taller than me, disgusting for the creator of the best investigative agency on the Twelve Stations. Short cut, bristly brown hair tops Terry's mountainous form. And I mean mountainous as in not a good place to climb rather than fat. His pale brown eyes stare out of a face that once bobbled with fat, until Carl and I did an intervention. We threatened Terry with no Gut-Buster Pizza for a year unless he got in shape. Shocking, I knew at the time, but the tactic worked. With no choice other than eating his dad's chancy cooking, he took off weight and muscled up. A couple of girls approached him on the promenade last week. Blushing, he backed off fast but kept looking at one of them.

"Luxury level, Suite A-781," I say and explain the case after the lift accepts the command. "Sounds pretty simple. Shouldn't take more than an hour."

Yeah. Right.

Nothing is simple on Canoples Station, especially in 2364. More visitors than ever visit since scientists predicted the massive volcano on Io will experience its biggest eruption ever soon – soon being ten minutes from now to maybe a year or more.

"Nearly there," Carl says.

"Yeah." I watch the last three numbers flash. "Uh. Forgot to mention something."

The lift stops.

"What?" Terry asks.

"Our client thinks someone tossed her bag into one of the garbage chutes," I say. "We'll have to start in the skin zone."

The lift doors slide open but not fast enough. Carl's fists open and close. Terry stares at me open-mouthed.

"The skin zone!" both of them shout. "Are you mental?"

There is some truth to that. Anyone willing to go into the skin zone has to be a little mental. Just a little, but no way will they get away with calling me mental.

"No more than you," I say. "You're my backup."

They lunge at me.

CHAPTER THREE

Wordless roars pursue me along the corridor, but I have one thing Carl and Terry lack – quick feet. Years of practice avoiding my big bro taught me more than a few tricks.

"Stop!" Carl shouts.

"Wait, BD," Terry yells.

I dart through an access hatch. They catch up to me as I straddle a railing.

"Didn't you read today's safety flash?" Carl's voice squeaks. "Maintenance is realigning the gravity nets!"

Gravity nets are a safety feature anywhere on the station where the possibility of falling more than five feet exists. The skin zone has nothing but girders crisscrossing the space between the station's covering and the living areas. There are thirty-five main levels, and three sub-levels – about thirty-five hundred feet from the top of the station to the bottom. After factoring in the vents and Jeffries tubes …

Who bothers with a safety flash? Do what I have to, enjoy myself all the time, what other way is there to live?

The annoying notices bore me to tears because there are so many of them. But I vow to pay more attention to them in the future with the air-driven safety nets down when we need them.

Time for Plan B.

Forget about asking what Plan B is; I always figure it out on the fly. Looking down, I search nearby girders for our quarry and come close to hurling every meal I've ever eaten. The grossest bag in creation dangles from a girder below me. According to the description in the i-mail, this is what our client wants.

Now, I'm not much on women's fashions. Honestly, I never think about them. Due to the remote possibility of decompression, everyone wears jumpsuits with survival gear built into them. A few girls experiment with baubles they hang off their ears or in their hair, but no one gets to choose the color of their jumpsuits; the ruling council makes that decision for each station. On Canoples, we wear silver jumpsuits. Security wears the pukey green color no matter what station they serve on, a situation I never lose a chance to tease Wade about. Although, I might have to stop doing that since I'll have to wear one of those awful jumpsuits as soon as I go to the Security Academy.

"We're after that." I point at the bag. "Grab my feet if I slip."

Safety first! Of course, I have a very good reason. Seeing my mom's face when EMTs carry me into emergency is a first on every things-to-avoid list I've ever made. The thought of one of her what-were-you-thinking lectures keeps me on the straight and narrow, as I define straight and narrow.

"That's the ugliest thing in the galaxy," Terry says.

"You won't catch me touching it." Carl shudders. "It looks like something the garbage chute regurgitated."

Elected by disgust, I hang upside down from a girder while reaching for an orange, purple, and yellow travel bag. How it ended up dangling between the skin zone and living areas is far beyond me.

"Watch out!" Carl shouts.

Not the first time I hear a warning, and probably not the last. We always bring back what our client wants, no matter what we have to do. Our antics usually leave me digging for an explanation when Security hears about them.

Seconds after the warning comes, I understand why. *Oh, boy. I'm in real trouble now!* The slick fabric of my jumpsuit slides a micrometer.

I'll worry about that later. Gotta get that bag so we have enough creds for Asteroids. "Almost have it," I holler.

And hope with every fiber of my being my buds keep me from taking a header into the bowels of the station. No one, except a couple of guys in maintenance and Station Security, knows what's down there. While we never worry about working up high, we will never breach those access hatches.

To say I never want to make that discovery is like saying no one willingly takes a dive out an airlock without protective gear. Let the junk stay where it is. Whatever is down there has nothing to do with my current objective, which is to get the bag the wife of Rendall Station's governor when traveling, back.

My fingers grip the strap as my knees slide forward even more.

Fear locks my heart in place. It's in my throat. I look at the bottom of the station, thirty-five levels below me. There are plenty of girders between me and bouncing off the steel deck. With my current position, I will body check every single one on my way down.

"Gotcha!" Terry yells.

Two hands grab my ankles. Seconds later, a cred chip slides out of my pocket and plummets past my face. Sweat pops out on my forehead.

That could have been me!

"Pulling you up," Carl says.

Inch by jerking inch, I move backward. While I want to check out how Carl and Terry are dragging me to safety, or in my case, keeping my mom from yelling until doomsday about putting myself in danger, I stare at a bright green light blinking below me.

"Hold up," I call.

"Are you freakin' nuts?" Carl demands. "We're barely holding onto you now. What are you eating? You weigh almost as much as Jake."

That's an insult of the highest degree. Jake Tigley hangs out with Lisa Tulane. Both spend a great deal of time scarfing down everything sweet on the station and giving us a hard time. Oh, and both resemble one of those elephants from Earth, big and lumbering.

"Don't insult me," I shout back. "I haven't gained that much." Well, it is a bit of a stretch. My appetite, never small, took off since my birthday almost a year ago but then, so has my height, but I'm still as wiry as always. "Give me a minute to check this out."

"Don't take too long," Terry says.

I stop moving long enough to figure out whatever caught my attention doesn't look important.

Maybe. Or maybe not. Don't let it be what I think it is. No way could someone be down there. I'm not seeing a locater beacon. Nope. Just my imagination.

"Okay, pull me up."

The journey upward continues until I lay on the catwalk between Carl and Terry.

"What did you see?" Carl asks.

"Don't know." I roll over and glance down. "It's not very big. Looks like it's blinking."

"A locater beacon," Terry says, making me wince when he voices my earlier thought.

"Might be," I say, and groan silently. *This is not what we need.*

Everyone on the Twelve Stations wears a locator beacon. In the event of an emergency, Security can find us without dedicating resources to a search. It hasn't always been this way, but during a meteorite penetration evacuation exercise, a few teens failed to show up at their reporting area – me and the guys. We had discovered a pile of counterfeit creds in a storage room. When the klaxon blew, we refused to stop prying the creds out of their hiding place, and were so determined to turn them in for the reward we never thought about getting to our designated shelter.

Even though Carl, Terry, and I got the grounding of our lives, six weeks of my older brother shadowing us like we were three, we pursued our passion with Carl's twin, Cassie. She gave up what she calls nasty, dirty idiocy to hang out with some girls from the high school.

I concentrate on the blinking below me. Sound drifts past the usual station noises and I know, without any doubts, we have trouble. This is the kind of trouble ensuring the death of Canoples Investigations if we fail to report it immediately.

"Did someone just yell for help?" Carl comes to his feet and leans over the railing.

"Sure sounds like it." Terry joins him.

"Great." I stalk toward the access door. "Call Security and have them meet us at Governor Jackson's quarters. We still have to unload this bag."

Like I want to hold onto something so stupid looking. I have no idea who designed women's fashions, but they must have found them in a space dust nightmare. Just looking at the travel bag makes me want to swear off Gut-Buster Pizza the rest of my life.

My buds behind me, I storm onto the luxury suite level and bolt toward the largest one at the end of the corridor. Two beefy-looking guys stop us before we reach the door.

"Canoples Investigations returning Mrs. Jackson's bag," I say. "She wanted us to give it to her ourselves."

"Sure, kid," beefy guy on the right says. "Hand it over."

"Really." I tighten my fingers around the strap. "Mrs. Jackson told me to make sure nothing happened to her bag. How can I do that if you take it from me?"

Okay, stretching the truth a little. Mrs. Jackson's i-mail said she lost an important bag. I figure it's worth a shot, and maybe a great tip, if I give it back.

Beefy guy on the left scratches his ear. Together, these guys look like they strain to read an interactive pre-school vid-book. How much brainpower does someone need to protect the most scandal-riddled governor of the Twelve Stations?

Not much. Lots of muscle but no brains.

"Wait here."

The first beefy guy leans through the door. I try with all my might to see what is so interesting about those people. Both are stick thin. They wear purplish jumpsuits signifying they belong to the ruling council. More importantly, they have the creds to keep my buds and me in snacks after we pick up our new game.

"Yo, BD," Terry whispers. "Security's on the way now. Hurry up."

Oh, like I want to hang around here all day.

Canoples Investigations has a lot more important things to do. One, me convincing Cassie to stop glaring lasers through me with each glance.

Splitting the back of my jumpsuit, laughing after she told me about making the cheerleading squad, started the cold war. The day I teased her for acting like a girl heated up the action. Her glares hurt, but I will never tell her I'm sorry.

Maybe.

CHAPTER FOUR

Never before having had a reason to come up to the luxury level, I put my wait for Mrs. Jackson to good use. All investigators take in their surroundings for future reference. My brother taught me that particular bit of information, but Dad had snorted at the advice, and then he had told me to forget Security as a career. He thought I needed to explore asteroid mining. Those companies pull in mountains of creds while blasting rocks and collecting all kinds of ores.

Oh yeah! Like I really want to sit around all day pushing buttons. I might do almost anything for creds, but I'll never run an asteroid miner. Boring!

In my opinion – *the only one that counts* –, those pilots are optional. An engineer will figure out a way for the computer to fly an asteroid miner one day, and then all those guys will have to train for another job.

The beefy guys blocking the entrance to the Jackson's suite move closer together, taking my mind off Dad's dumb advice. An image flits into my memory banks, one triggered by a babysitting nightmare, involving multiple three-year-olds. There is no way in the galaxy I want to remember this particular image. I raise my eyebrows and wrinkle my nose at how much these bodyguards look like Gorg and Ebo, a pair of klutzy space explorers little kids go ga-ga over. Beefy guy number one resembles Gorg with lots of facial hair and dark skin. Beefy guy number two is kind of pale with deep green eyes and almost white hair, an exact duplicate of Ebo, right down to the half-goofy, half-stupid expression on his face.

"What's up, Gorg?" I ask beefy guy number one. "Do you think I'll try to rush you?"

In a Mercury second, if I think I can get past the two of you.

The Gorg and Ebo lookalikes move as one. They fold their arms across their chests and squint at me. I can't help cracking up.

"So, did you find Sugar Tree Haunt, Ebo?" I ask.

No way it can happen, but Gorg and Ebo, as I now think of them, look even more confused.

Come on! Don't tell me these rejects from a garbage scow don't know about the greatest hunt Gorg and Ebo went on, just so all those parents would approve a sixty-cred charge for their kids to watch the movie?

Snickers behind me indicate Carl and Terry are enjoying the teasing as much as I am. Some might say I'm bullying these two men. I see this as an opportunity to test how far I can go before they leave their post, and give me a great opportunity to sneak inside.

Then, shame washes through me. One thing my dad taught me was to never tease or bully someone who isn't as smart as me. Of course, obeying the old instruction leaves out most of the best targets, but I haven't acted like this in ages.

Thinking about Dad brings up feelings I would rather ignore so I focus on the luxury level. All of the large suites will easily accommodate three families. Carl passed on that bit of information after Cassie chased him out of their shared bathroom a year back. She claimed he smelled it up. Unfortunately, no one living on Canoples can rent one of these places while waiting for a larger unit, or in Carl's case, one with a second bathroom.

Tourism is what makes creds for Canoples. The luxury level and the three levels below it are for tourists only, leaving the rest of us stuck in cramped quarters. The weird lavender color on the walls fascinates me, but I keep an ear tuned to the Jackson's suite. Long strips of lights set into where the walls join the ceiling and floor provides muted illumination. Still-vids break up the long walls between suites, all of them scenes of Jupiter. Some are what we see from the station while others are of the areas on the planet safe to visit. None is anything new, and my attention wanders.

"BD," Carl says in a low voice. "What's taking so long?"

"Don't know." I glance at Gorg and Ebo, wondering if I can make a break past them and get inside the suite. Both stare straight ahead and stand like two massive statues. "We can't leave."

Not with this stupid travel bag still in my hand. Anyone seeing me with it will tease me until shame kills me. Bouncing from foot to foot keeps me from going nuts while waiting to see who will arrive first, Station Security or Mrs. Jackson. To my relief, my client glides out the open door and makes a beeline for me.

"You found Chuckles," she cries in a whispery voice.

She calls her travel bag Chuckles? My already low opinion of anti-station freaks and politicians drops lower than Pluto's temperature. The very idea of naming a travel bag is bad enough, but to call it *Chuckles*. Get real!

Carl and Terry will never let me live this down. Checking to make sure they aren't close, I glance over a shoulder. They grin at me from two feet away.

Humiliation on the way! This is not my most embarrassing moment, but it comes close.

"Yes, ma'am," I say in my most respectful voice, even though I want to do nothing more than shove the bag into her flabby arms and run for my life. "Chuckles is fine."

"How do you know?" she screeches. "Did you disturb him?"

"No, ma'am." I hand her the bag. "I found it in the skin zone. Chuckles looks okay. Not even a scratch."

"What do you mean you found him in the skin zone?" Her fingers work the clasp. "How did he get there?"

"You said in your i-mail you might have left it near a garbage chute." I shrug. "You're lucky someone tossed Chuckles into the chute instead of reporting an abandoned bag. Security spaces those."

Whoa! Hold on. My explanation might make sense to someone with half a brain, but it bothers me. Stuff dumped in the garbage chute comes out in the recycle center. It never ends up in the skin zone, unless a breach opens in a tube.

"Who would do such an awful thing?" Her whiny voice rises to a squeal. "Who would destroy my property?"

Gorg and Ebo grin and look away fast. I have my suspicions. Their grins give them away. Since they messed up my fun, I decide to make them nervous.

"My older brother works for Station Security," I say. "He told me this kind of crime is usually done by someone close to the victim."

The personal guards stare at me with looks of horror. Mrs. Jackson's face pales to an almost greenish color.

"You can't know that." She opens the bag. "Oh! Chuckles, baby. Did those nasty boys hurt you?"

A funny noise answers her; a noise sounding like a cross between a rumble and humming. My eyes widen. Bringing anything live onto a station requires a permit. I shoot Terry and Carl a worried look. They take off for the lift, Carl holding his PocketPad in front of him. The miniature computer glows blue, and I hope they have called Security to report the violation. No way do I want trouble for helping someone break the rules.

Fear of losing income isn't the only reason. My buds and I might take chances. We push limits we think are silly, but we never outright break the rules. Mom's disappointment is only a small part of what keeps me in line. How I feel inside is the biggest reason. Sneaking around, living on the edge, always wondering when Security will catch me, none of that is worth the risk.

I open my mouth, to confront Mrs. Jackson about what I heard. She stares inside the cavernous bag.

"Mommy's here, baby," she croons. "We'll find the awful person who hid you from me."

She pulls out a re-kat, a cloned version of the house cats from Earth. They are disgusting creatures who make messes, eat, and sleep.

Who wants something so dumb? Not me!

This particular re-kat has orange and white zigzagged fur and gray eyes. It cuddles Mrs. Jackson while making the dumb noise. I guess it's a purr. Whatever it is, I want to get my creds and jet out of there before Security shows up. Their fine might change her mind about paying me for almost falling thirty-five hundred feet to save an illegal re-kat.

The sound of boots sliding across the floor diverts me. The governor joins the mess. He looks determined to stop me from doing my duty.

"How much does my wife owe you?" Governor Jackson asks.

I look up into his face. That's a real cute trick, since I am taller than almost everyone else on the station. The man stands almost seven feet. Humans have not grown so tall since the evacuation. He has broken more than a few laws, like taking steroids in addition to smuggling re-kats.

"Three hundred creds," I answer while hoping he hands the creds over fast. "I have the account information for the transfer."

"No need for an electronic trail." He digs into a pocket and pulls out a stack of credits. "What say I triple your usual fee?" He winks.

"We don't want the wrong people hearing about Chuckles. Do we?"

"No, sir."

Who am I to argue with getting nine hundred creds instead of three? Not me. No one can say BD Bradford is stupid.

Well, a few try. Most walk away with an earful of yelling but nothing else. I sure don't want Mom hearing about me getting into a fight. She can holler far better than me any day of the week.

Other consequences await anyone using physical violence. The least, giving up free time for a month to attend a class on controlling impulses. Then the offender has two hundred hours cleaning Jeffries tubes. I might crave excitement more than a Gut-Buster Pizza, but the thought of wiggling through crud-encrusted tubes squashes any desire to throw a punch.

The lift doors open. I check over my shoulder. Security is on the way, in the forms of Chief Pelham and Wade. Holding out my hand, I wait for the creds to slap my palm. The satisfying feel of chips against my skin comes as the governor counts.

"One hundred, two hundred." Governor Jackson pokes through the pile of cred chips in his hand.

Unless he put some moves into his stick-thin, icy fingers, I will find myself in the middle of a mess, and the money will be a long forgotten dream. Then I stop worrying about getting the creds when I feel more hitting my palm.

"Seven hundred, eight hundred, and nine hundred," he says. "Thanks for bringing back Chuckles. Sweetums couldn't sleep a wink last night thinking something awful had happened to him."

Is he in for a surprise, along with his wife and the re-kat. Quarantine means a month locked up in a cage without visits from the owner. *Poor Chuckles – not! He will probably enjoy the break.*

"Not a problem." Like I'll tell him it is. "Contact us on Canoples 872 if you need anything else." *Please don't!* "Canoples Investigations always locates their quarry," I tell him our motto, hoping he never calls.

CHAPTER FIVE

I can't make my feet move fast enough to get away from the scene, and none too soon. Chief John Pelham and my older-but-far-stupider brother, Wade, zero in on the re-kat.

"Stand fast, BD," Chief Pelham orders. "I want to know what your involvement is."

Oh yeah. Involvement. Not something I look forward to explaining. A couple of inches taller than me, he took over Security after my dad's disappearance. The chief's trim and muscular body makes an impression on teens when they think about starting trouble. He goes out of his way to point kids in the right direction and refuses to play favorites with anyone, including those on the Ruling Council and Canoples' politicians. That more than anything makes me admire the man even though he gave my family the rotten news about Dad's death.

Wade smirks. "Looks like your business days are numbered, bro."

Can he be just a little more irritating? Hoppin' space rocks, I hope not. Mom hates it when we fight, which is every two seconds when we're together. She never believes me when I tell her it's his fault. He never leaves me alone.

"We need to talk," Chief Pelham says. "I didn't find a permit for the re-kat."

"What re-kat?" Governor Jackson asks.

His face reflecting innocent shock, he stands in front of his wife. She stuffs the protesting animal into the bag and shoves the ugly thing behind her back. The righteous look on her face makes me wonder how dumb she is. Everyone in the corridor has a very good look at where she stands. Mrs. Jackson may be skinny, but behind her husband she looks ten times wider than he is. And the re-kat's scratching and yowls fill the air. Good thing I have no idea what the animal says. From the ruckus it puts up, I can guess.

"We don't own a re-kat," she says. "Check the records on Rendall Station if you don't believe us."

My opinion of the Jacksons goes up a little. Not one other person I have ever come into contact with lies as well as they do.

"Your spacecraft logged a stop at Mistlich Station." Chief Pelham smiles. "Records there indicate you adopted an older re-kat named Chuckles."

Caught!

A ton of newscasts adding to the already black record the Jacksons have is in their future. Too bad it has to include my buds and me. We need advertising, just not how the vid-reporters will spin it. The Jackson's reputation for blaming others makes me cringe. I don't need that kind of trouble.

Fear rushes through me when they grin in my direction. *Nine hundred creds doesn't give them the right to blame me!* I will do whatever it takes to protect my name.

"That boy." Governor Jackson flicks a hand at me. "Brought us something I identified as contraband." He straightens until he towers over everyone. "I was just getting ready to notify you about his criminal activities."

A low growl rumbles from where Wade stands. Disbelief replaces my fear. Is my big brother about to defend me? This is worth sticking around to see. Wade hasn't stood up for me against anyone, not even once. But before he can speak, Chief Pelham shakes his head. All I can do is stare at the Jacksons.

"Really?" The chief raises an eyebrow. "Then please explain why I received vid of your wife asking about Chuckles? Is she clairvoyant?" He holds up a hand when the governor opens his mouth. "Don't bother with another lie. We have data confirming the i-mail she sent Canoples Investigations. Awful lot of fuss for something you claim you don't own."

"Kids today can fake anything," Governor Jackson claims. "That boy said he'd already created evidence to make me look bad."

"BD?" Wade snorts with laughter. "He can barely turn on a computer."

Why does he have to point out my less than stellar qualities?

Being my older brother doesn't give him the right, no matter how many times he says it does. The problem is not a lack of knowledge. Space station kids use computers from birth, but I like being different.

Refusing to acknowledge I know more than anyone else on Canoples except my buds about computers is the only way I can do it.

"I won't let you have my baby!"

Mrs. Jackson darts into their suite. The door whooshes closed. Seconds later, the sound of a lock engaging echoes throughout the corridor. I hoof it over to where Terry and Carl wait.

"He paid triple." I divide the booty. "The governor doesn't want us to say anything."

"He should have talked faster." Carl pockets his creds. "Great job, BD. What about that noise we heard in the skin zone."

I glance at the growing argument in front of the governor's quarters. Gorg and Ebo have taken up positions in front of the door. Both appear as if Wade and Chief Pelham will have to stun them to get inside the suite.

"It can wait." Terry leans against the wall. "I want to see the jerks get the treatment."

The most important station laws, no matter which one someone is on, are all the same. No importing of any kind of live animal without permits, no defying Security when they are on duty, and mostly, no private protection keeping Security from doing their job. The most scandalous governor in history has broken all of them.

"My wife can't go anywhere without Chuckles. She just got him. They've already bonded," Governor Jackson says. "The quarantine period would drive her insane. We're only here for a week. Can't you make an exception?"

"Have her unlock the door and bring out the re-kat," Chief Pelham says. "Right now, it's a fifteen hundred cred fine. If she persists in hiding the animal, we're talking about arrests and trials."

My palms tingle. Excitement rises. I want to join the fun but have to check out the voice I heard. Someone is in trouble deep within the station. Security is busy. Well, not all of them, but we can't wait for anyone else to respond. It is up to Canoples Investigations to save the day.

"You'll never take Chuckles from me," Mrs. Jackson hollers from behind the door. "Protect my baby, devoted Henrys."

Well, maybe the voice I heard can wait a minute or two. This sounds like it going to get good.

"Devoted Henrys?" I ask. "Don't tell me she hired two men with the same name."

"Nah." Carl smiles. "You know how Mom loves Inside Galaxy? They interviewed Mrs. Jackson last week. She said she can't remember names so she always calls her private protection Henry."

"I don't believe it," I say.

The sounds of two bodies hitting something hard makes me look at the Jackson's quarters. Henry 1, Gorg, slides down a wall. Henry 2, Ebo, lies in a heap on the deck. Chief Pelham inserts an override key-card into the lock and opens the door while Wade stands over the knocked out men.

"I want one of those key-cards," I whisper.

"Don't we all." Carl sounds as envious as me.

Wade runs inside and returns seconds later with a hissing, spitting Chuckles.

Security, and especially my bro, face all kinds of unusual situations. Arriving spaceships needing decontamination, breeched air locks, and kids investigating forbidden parts of the station are just a few. An angry re-kat held six inches from a human body with its claws stretched and paws swinging in an attempt to latch onto anything in its path is a first. So far as I know, Security lacks the restraints capable of defusing the damage those claws can cause.

"How will you restrain the prisoner?" I ask.

"Go play outside an airlock without protective gear," he says.

"Nice to know you care so much, but no thanks. I like living too much." I kick back against the wall. "I think I'll just hang around and see how you restrain your prisoner. It should make for great tales on the promenade later."

He shoots me a look promising retribution at a later, more private time and ducks when Mrs. Jackson beans him with her bag. Chuckles gets loose and scrambles back into the quarters; its claws destroying everything in its path. The governor jumps on Chief Pelham's back when he goes after the re-kat. Looking nothing like his usual perfect self, Wade dives through the door, barely avoiding the governor's kick.

No wonder everyone talks about the Jacksons!

CHAPTER SIX

Chief Pelham shrugs off the governor, but the two Henrys come around and dive into the altercation with fists swinging. Gorg and Ebo have certainly proved they are more than muscles upon muscles! They put their punches where they can draw the most damage. This is getting good! I decide I won't call them Gorg and Ebo anymore. They're not as dumb as they first appeared.

The men slam against a wall, and the corridor shakes. My buds and I back off a few feet. A couple of doors slide open behind us but then close real fast. *Neat trick.* The station's mainframe controls doors at a safe speed to prevent accidental crushings.

"Hand over the re-kat!" Wade shouts.

He's still inside the governor's suite. From all the thumps and thuds, it sounds like there's some really good action happening.

"Never!" Mrs. Jackson shrieks. "No one will ever take away my beloved Chuckles."

The re-kat howls and hisses. Seconds later, Wade tumbles out the door head over heels. She chases after him with the animal perched on her hair. Chuckles looks like a weird hat with its fur standing on end, and its tail wrapped around her neck.

"Sure hope no one calls the news-vids." Carl glances at the lifts. "This is probably the Jacksons' worst moment."

I follow his look, squinting to make sure none of the lifts have activated. No red glow appears next to the actuator pad, letting me breathe a little easier. The governor's attempt to blame me might have made no impression on Chief Pelham, but news-vid reporters never pay attention to the truth. Scandal in large doses attracts audiences, and the Jackson's always give them plenty.

"They tried to blame me," I say.

"We heard," Terry says, watching the action. "The news-vids will get this; as soon as we make sure no one blames us." He holds up his PocketPad with the vid function activated. "I decided to record this particular encounter, just in case the Jackson's tried to blame C.I."

"Good." I focus on the action at the other end of the corridor. "Wish I'd thought of it."

"Nah. Governor Jackson can't blame you this way." He whoops. "Go for it, Wade."

I smile when my big brother scrambles free of Mrs. Jackson's talon like fingers. She darts back into the suite. Her silly smacks against the wall almost make me laugh. She has no idea how futile her actions are. Once Security uses an override key-card, the door remains open until Control deactivates the card. That will happen as soon as she releases her contraband.

Never, not the way they're acting.

"We really should check out the skin zone," Carl says.

His voice sounds like nothing will move him from where we stand, not even a meteorite penetrating the station's skin. Me either. Not once in my memory have I heard about someone fighting Security. Given the chance to witness the violation in person, I have to stick around.

"What if that person is in bad trouble?" Terry asks.

Guilt nibbles at my conscience. I'm not responsible for rescuing someone in trouble. Security is. The locator band board controller must have fallen asleep. As far as I know, no one has gone to check out the signal yet.

"Did you tell Chief Pelham what we saw?" I ask.

"Sort of." Carl says. "I told him something strange was down there since we weren't sure."

"Oh," I silently cheer Wade.

He knocks out one of the Henrys. Given the guy stands half a foot taller and outweighs my brother by close to a hundred pounds it takes some doing.

"We should check it out," I say.

I glance at Terry and Carl before nodding at a nearby airshaft. Silent agreement evident on their faces, we sidle toward the fastest method of transportation on the station.

"Gotta move it," I mumble. "That person can't last much longer. It's almost time for a sweep."

Sweep refers to the daily clearing of all trash accumulated in the skin zone. If someone from Maintenance doesn't run the magnets through there, a piece of junk might pierce the skin. Then all of our oxygen will escape.

"Do we have to use the air shaft?" Terry asks.

He hates tight spaces. Not that I blame him, but speed is of the essence. Carl stands lookout while I loosen the grate.

Whoever last inspected the grate torqued down when they tightened the screws. I pull out my multi-tool and apply a lot of muscle before anything happens. The first three come out without too much of a problem. The fourth screeches a protest, making me wince and check out the action at the Jackson's suite. Everyone down there is still fighting for control of the re-kat.

"Need a diversion," I whisper.

"Coming up," Terry says. "Give me the word when you're ready."

He shudders and moves to one side. Back in kindergarten, when he was a little taller and heavier than the rest of the class, he found himself locked in a storage unit by Jake. Terry had been so scared he could not move let alone call out. Our teacher found him when she went to get fingerpaint.

The reluctance in his voice gives me an idea.

"Why don't you hang with the chief and Wade?" I suggest. "Make sure the governor believes we didn't rat out his wife. Never know if they'll need something else."

I shudder at the thought. But then, creds are creds, no matter who pays them.

"Great idea," he says.

"Go ahead and get in position," I tell him. "I'm almost ready here."

Terry runs along the corridor. While he has been a real klutz most of his life, recently he shaped up. With the reputation of Canoples Investigations on the line, I'm sure he will come through for us.

"Cassie wants to talk to you," Carl says. "What did you do now?"

"Nothing." I keep an eye on Terry, wondering when he will make his move.

"She sounded hot this morning when she heard your name," Carl says. "It happened right after the news finished."

"Oh, that." My mind sends commands to Terry to make his move. "Explain later. Why is Cassie upset anyway? It's not like she took her name off our business license."

Twelve Stations allows teens to run their own business, as soon as they turn fourteen and have a parent's permission. All of ours gave it willingly. They thought it was a good way to keep us out of trouble.

"Yeah." Carl grins. "I reminded her about that. She said she'd fix it later."

"Let her." I grab his arm. "Get ready."

In fabulous fashion, Terry skids into the governor. Governor Jackson's arms windmill as he stumbles backward. Both Henrys have just picked themselves up off the deck for the second time. Their boss slams into them, and they tumble to the floor. The pileup slides away from the door. Wade and Chief Pelham push the still shrieking Mrs. Jackson aside.

"Now," I whisper.

Carl pulls off the grate. We crawl inside and brace ourselves against the tunnel. After he pushes the grate back into place, we balance over the downward spiraling hole.

"Any time you're ready," he says.

"Bombs away!"

I read the expression in a history vid-book and think it sounds great. Bending my knees, I jump. About a second later, I remember something.

"Did that safety flash mean the tubes, too?" I yell.

"Don't remember."

My eyes widen. Carl is too close for me to make an attempt to slow down. I bend my knees to soften the landing and hope the pain of him slamming into me isn't too intense. Three flights later, I land on the safety cushion installed to keep kids from hurting themselves riding the tubes. A whoop makes me realize how little time I have to clear the spot. I roll left as he bounces off the pad a couple of times. He hits the air cushion only micrometers from me!

"Guess no one shut them off." He takes off at a run. "Race you for the next one."

"Cheater!" I chase after him.

Another safety feature, airshafts only go three levels, and then they move to another area. Life is so safe on Canoples, and all the Twelve Stations, we have to work hard to skin a knee or elbow. I long ago figured out why but not how to change it.

According to what I learned about kids on Earth, they took all kinds of chances and spent a lot of time healing from injuries. Then adults started making them wear protective gear. Of course, the kids got rid of the gear as fast as they could.

We have no choice on a space station. No matter what we do, adults have already figured out a way to keep us safe. Well, most of us. My buds and I tend to go places other teens avoid.

Carl and I find the next airshaft. We keep going until we reach the bottom. A massive gray door looms in front of us. Shoving aside the sensible voice in my head telling me to back off, I dart into the skin zone.

"Where to now?" I ask, looking in all directions.

"Not sure," he says.

If we were inside the station instead of next to the skin, we could have consulted one of the many vid-maps on the walls. As it is, we are stuck figuring out where the locater beacon is.

"Guess we do it the hard way," I say.

"Ain't that the truth." He grins. "But it's so much more fun."

He sure has that right. We have the most fun when we do things the way no one else will. Except this time, I hate the thought of tromping around, worrying about when the magnets will activate.

"Better put some moves into it," I say. "I sure don't want to explain to Chief Pelham why we didn't tell him about this."

Carl goes left, and I take off to the right. No words are necessary. Both of us realize the urgency of finding the locator beacon and making sure no one is with it.

Boy, I will blast the ears off the kid who left their locator beacon in a place where it would end up down here. Talk about incredibly stupid.

Nerves make me as jumpy as Chuckles. We have a huge area to search and very little time. With my ears fine-tuned to catch the first indication of the sweep, I move in a zigzag pattern. There is enough junk around my boots to make several recyclers happy for months.

"What happened to disposing of this stuff properly?" I whisper.

This place gives me the creeps, a first I never thought I would experience. Even when my dad told stories about the Jupiter Man-Monsters, I laughed instead of screaming in terror. Not much puts fear bumps on my skin, but this place does. Maybe it has a lot to do with how close I am to the cold darkness of space. Or maybe this is just the creepiest place I have ever encountered. Whatever it is, I want to find the source of that locater beacon and beat feet back inside the station.

I check for Carl. He is near the other side of the station, but I can only tell that by how his jumpsuit brightens the murky light.

"This is so dumb." I shove aside a travel bag uglier than Mrs. Jackson's. "We should have told the chief."

This would have taken forever to explain, not to mention listening to Wade's lecture about staying out of the skin zone. I reach for a broken girder, to move it aside.

"Over here," Carl hollers. "It's a little girl."

Magnetic clamps begin to lock down the exits and airshafts. My blood runs cold.

Out of time! Now what?

CHAPTER SEVEN

The deep clang-clang-thud continues in a slow, ear splitting procession. Programmed into the station's mainframe, the procedure starts on the upper luxury level, where the Jacksons are currently trying to avoid giving up Chuckles. Doors above us thump into place, coming closer and closer as they shut and seal. Inside the station, an announcement will advise everyone to stay away from the skin access hatches. Most people barely hear it, even me. Until today, when I want a computer glitch, a rare occurrence, to stop the process before it reaches us.

No such luck. I curse my rotten luck. Maintenance has messed up big time. Before starting the procedure, dispatch has to turn on the remote cameras and make sure no one is inside the skin zone. Carl and I remained in plain sight during our search. Three of those remote cameras pinpoint our position right now, but they are in rest mode, lying among the junk, and we cannot rely on Terry revealing our plan once he hears the announcement.

With no idea how to get out of our current mess, I cannot move fast enough to find Carl and the little girl. Once the clamps lock down, no one can get in or out until after the trash has been spaced.

CANOPLES INVESTIGATIONS TACKLES SPACE PIRATES

The situation brings icy fear to anyone living on a space station. Spaced means flying into the black coldness without protection. We only have seconds to unlock the clamps before the sweep begins, and our computer expert is thirty-five floors above us keeping Security occupied.

"Wonderful planning." I skid around a corner as a hum fills the air. "Find an access hatch. We're in trouble."

"Ya think?" Carl's voice is close.

Running faster, I find him trying to pick up a little girl who looks like she is three. Her locater is on her upper arm, the usual spot for small kids so they cannot accidentally pull it off. Her head spins in all directions, and her eyes are wide with terror. One of her hands reaches for a corner where a pile of junk lies against the wall.

"No time to find your cuddle toy," I say. "How did you get in here?"

Tears puddle in her eyes. Her lower lip trembles, but she doesn't say a word.

"Come on, kid," I beg. "That door might still be open. We have to get out of here."

She sticks a thumb into her mouth. Tears roll down her pudgy cheeks, and a sad little whimper makes me feel like the worst jerk in the galaxy. Not enough of a jerk to take the time to find her cuddle toy. Lives are at stake. Our lives.

"Please?" I say in my nicest voice. "It's not safe to stick around here. Can't you help us?"

The kid plants her butt on the junk covering the deck. More tears race down her cheeks, and the whimper becomes a frightened wail.

"Give your PocketPad a shot," Carl says, desperation in his voice. "I'll carry the kid. We have to get out of here now. I don't want to end up outside the station."

We only have a mili-second for his suggestion to work. I glance at the wall, make a guess, and send the location to both Security and Maintenance.

Sure hope this works.

After what seems like a lifetime, the hum stops. No vibration comes, which means we might have notified the right people someone is in the skin zone. Carl grabs the kid and holds her tight against his chest. She responds much like Chuckles did on the luxury level, kicking and screaming.

Boy, for such a small kid, she sure makes a lot of noise.

"Let's go." I run toward an access door. "Don't drop her. We're still in trouble."

The door opens when we are still two feet from it. No worries there. My emergency notification activated a rescue response built into the station's computers. We burst into the corridor, to the grinning faces of a Security team led by Hank Graham.

No matter where we are on the station, he shows up every time we find ourselves in a tight spot. This is beyond bad. I have to explain everything now, which includes the triple fee we just scored.

I can just see my Asteroids game going right out a porthole. Talk about messed up. My troubles have only just begun.

"Well, if it isn't BD Bradford and his sidekick, Carl Wills," Graham says. "Where's the other one? The fat kid, Terry Ashley? He's usually with you."

Calling Terry fat is wrong. Sure, he had problems as a kid, but since our intervention, he muscled up. He is still big, but only an idiot upsets him now. Terry has a pretty good defense mechanism; he sits on whoever pisses him off.

"Terry?" I look at Carl and grin. "Do you remember where we left him?"

"Yup." He returns my grin. "He's helping the chief with that quarantine problem up top. You remember, the one where Governor Jackson's wife smuggled a re-kat on to Canoples. I bet Chief Pelham's looking for us right now."

He sets the kid on the deck. She starts for the access door, but I grab her arm and hold on tight. A wordless wail bursts out of her, and she yanks against my grip. Talk about determined! Carl and I risk our necks to save her, and she wants to go right back into the skin zone for her cuddle toy.

Maybe I'm guessing wrong, but my experience with little kids leaves me with the impression they can't move an inch without the stuffed toy that emits a soothing sound. Cuddle toys often help a child fall asleep when nothing else will.

Her crying bounces off the walls and echoes around everyone, and she is much louder than she was in the skin zone. Without exception, we all wince. Kids sure can make a lot of noise for something so small.

"Pelham knows where you are?" Graham asks.

"He does now." Carl holds up his PocketPad. "And he wants a full report about the situation."

Graham's smug look vanishes. Since my dad's death, he dreads confrontations with Pelham. For a very good reason. Women all over the station complain about how Graham files false reports about them after they tell him to get lost. He stays in trouble about his attitude all the time.

"Fink," Graham snaps. "I'll prove you snuck into the skin zone to make trouble." He indicates the half dozen men behind him. "They'll back me up."

"I'm sure they will." I look over the men and nod. "You always have at least one of them around to lie for you after a woman tells you your face looks like a million miles of asteroid damage."

His face turns a dark purple color, and his eyes bug out. The kid wails louder, the sound piercing through my brain. That pain I will take. I happen to agree with her. This guy looks like a walking space dust nightmare.

"The kid comes with me," he says.

He reaches for the girl. She reacts like all little kids around him. After kicking his leg, she holds onto mine and peeks around my knee.

It is almost too funny not to react, but I hold in my laughter. We are already in hot steam for slipping back inside the skin zone without letting Pelham know. Ridiculing one of his officers guarantees I'll make things worse.

Thing is, I cannot help myself. Even when Dad ran Security, Graham made me mad.

"Great technique," I say. "Did you really think it stood a chance?"

"Turn over the kid," Graham says. "I'm sure her parents are going nuts."

Does he really think telling me what to do will work? Maybe for Pelham. Once in a century for Wade. When I agree with my buds. Usually for Mom, but only because I hate her punishments. Everyone else falls into the not happening in my lifetime category. Graham will never have my agreement. Not sure why, but he makes my skin crawl.

"I'm not keeping her," I point out. "She hid behind me. Maybe she doesn't like your face.

Graham's face scares space ghouls. Since the Chemistry lab explosion last year, it turned even uglier. He puffs up and reaches for the kid again, his hand almost grabbing her hair. She snaps her teeth around his fingers and smacks them together hard enough to make me wince.

"Brat!" he hollers. "I'll fine your parents out of existence. You're spending a week in therapy for that."

"Ah don't do that," I say. "She's scared. You made it worse by not using her safe word. Do you even know what it is?"

He growls when Carl snickers. I slap a hand over my mouth to hold back any other witty comments.

Safe words are one of the first things kids learn. It means they can go with the adult talking to them. Security has one for every kid on the station, including visitors, so they can return them to their parents.

"Did she tell you her name?" another officer asks.

I lean to one side to check out who it is, although I already suspect. When one is around, the other is not far off. At times, I wonder if they have a thing going. Then have the same reaction that always goes through me as a visual forms.

Nasty! Yuck!

Space station residents don't make a huge issue about personal relationships, but I cannot handle the thought. It is just plain wrong.

An even uglier face comes into view. A huge smile sends my temper into a slow boil.

Yup. Hearing has not gone wonky from the visit to the skin zone. Sure is Brad Carson. When my dad went missing five years ago, he led the search. All he came back with were pieces of the flitter Dad used to check the area between Canoples and Jupiter for pirates.

Because of Carson, no one spent any more time looking for my dad. That makes me determined to find out what really happened as soon as I turn eighteen, when I can search without having to explain to everyone what I'm doing.

CHAPTER EIGHT

Carson wiggles a finger in a silent come here command at the little girl. She tightens her grip on my knee with one hand and grabs my jumpsuit with the other, right below the butt. The slick fabric bunches up between my legs. Movement becomes impossible. I'll fall on top of her if I take a step.

"Get over here, kid," he orders.

Can he growl just a little meaner? The kid hanging onto my knee has yet to cut off all the circulation. For such a small thing, she sure has a strong grip. Light red hair frames a sweet looking face. Chubby cheeks and huge blue eyes give her the appearance of Bu-Bu the Venutian, one of the most popular cuddle toys, but there is nothing cute about this child. Shaking, she presses against my leg.

"Bad man," she lisps.

We agree about that, but we have a bigger problem than lack of trust. Just what it is eludes me. I lean over and put my hands under her arms. Carl looks from us to Carson.

"We need the chief down here," Carl says. "This doesn't look good."

"Got that straight." I pick up the kid. "Tell him to meet us at our office."

Now, I have good reason to think Carson and his sidekick, Graham, are rotten. Telling me that my dad killed himself and the security patrol with him makes me mad. The way they dropped the information still annoys me, like I have to accept their superior knowledge and shut up. Carson and Graham laughed when I yelled that they were liars. They even had the nerve to call me a spoiled brat!

For seven long years, I have never forgotten the day they told me I no longer had a dad. Yet this kid I have never seen before identifies Carson as someone she wants nowhere near her. That needs an explanation, and I have no idea if she will open up with all those uniforms around, but I have to give it a shot.

"He's not a bad man." I hug her and hope I'm not opening a major scandal.

Not what Chief Pelham wants or needs, and I respect the man for taking over Dad's job without making me feel left out of important stuff he used tell me about. The major consequences of a report to Internal Security from the kid's parents, when we find them, makes me cringe.

Until last year, Station Security operated without a committee looking into how they handled their jobs. Then Governor Jackson's administration admitted they let his friends' sons and daughters handle the safety of Rendall Station. A bigger group of morons exists nowhere else in the galaxy. The General Council, kind of like the old United States' government but with more controls, created Internal

Security Division. Each station sends two officers on a five-year rotation to Aldebbaran, the galaxy's capital, to check on unexplainable incidents. They found nothing until an angry pilot filed a report about Security on the capital.

Those officers ran a counterfeit gem smuggling operation right under everyone's noses! Some of the government reps bought their stuff at ridiculously low prices. That happened six months ago, and the trials ended last week. Wade switched off the vid after listening to the newsreader announce everyone involved received a ten-year sentence on Fomalhaut. Then he said he hoped nothing else goes wrong with any security unit for a long time. Internal Security Division threatened to replace everyone, no matter who they are or what station they are on, if they even sniff a bad problem.

This tiny kid clinging to me has indicated one of Canoples' Security officers is a bad man. While I agree with her, I have to keep her quiet until Chief Pelham shows up.

"Really," I whisper. "He's ugly, not bad."

"Is bad." She snuggles her face against my neck.

"Nah." I pry her free. "See, he's wearing the pukey green uniform. That means he helps you."

"Bad man," the little girl repeats. "He push Mommy and Daddy into bad place."

"Where?" I ask.

Right at that second, the magnetic clamps work back into position. Certainty slithers up my spine, and I spin around but not before catching sight of the evil grins on Carson and Graham's faces.

"Override on the fly. Let the chief know we're in trouble." I shift the kid to my back. "Hang on."

While running for my life, I hear Carl complying with my request.

"7-Alpha-Bravo-Charlie-1," he says. "Shut down sweep. Repeat, 7-Alpha-Bravo-Charlie-1. Shut down sweep immediately. Chief Pelham meet Canoples Investigations in Stairwell Three."

The girl giggles and almost chokes me.

Ah gee! If I knew letting her cut off my air supply would make her feel safe, I would have done this in the skin zone.

"Thanks," I pant.

"You can't use that code," Graham yells. "It's restricted for Security use only."

Oh yeah. I know, but I swiped a copy of the station's emergency codes a couple of months ago when Wade left his book lying around. Me and the guys never used the codes before. Since we did it in front of a bunch of official witnesses, we probably won't get another chance to dodge trouble with them.

My feet pound along the corridor as I search for the right stairwell. To my horror, the sound of pursuit comes closer and closer with every passing microsecond. I push myself harder; strive for more speed, but I start slowing down. The little girls slips, and I fight to pull her back into place.

"Weeeee!" she squeals.

Oh, great. Now she thinks I'm her favorite toy.

I grab her hands and yank hard. The move lets me breathe a little easier, and I put as much speed as I can into my feet. Carl reaches the stairwell first and holds the door for me. Once we get inside, he fiddles with the lock until it shoots into place, and then he double twists the handle in the wrong direction. A loud crack echoes around us, hopefully meaning the latch broke. A grin spreads my lips when I hear bellows on the other side.

"Better hoof it," he says. "Terry didn't get a chance to test this. I don't know how long it'll hold them."

Racing up stairs with a child on my back is hard but not as difficult as others might think it is. Carl, Terry, and I are on the high school SpaceBall team. We spend hours working out. Not that it's necessary with the zero-G environment we play in, but it improves our game. Still, after ten floors, I'm beginning to find it hard to catch my breath. Cramps attack my legs with a ferocity I have never before experienced, slowing me to a crawl.

"Give her to me," Carl says.

"Want BD," the girl says. "He take care of kids."

Where does that come from? Sure I found a few lost kids but not for a couple of years. This girl would have still been an infant the last time I pulled a child off a girder before they plummeted to the deck.

"BD needs a break," I say. "Carl is good at catching kids, too. Wanna see?"

A deep thud below us tells me I have very little time to convince her. I pull the girl around, make sure she isn't scared, and toss her to

Carl. He swings her onto his back and takes off up the stairs with me right behind them. To my undying relief, I hear footsteps racing toward us from above.

"Better hurry," I yell. "They're right behind us."

"Where are you?" Wade yells.

"Fifteen." My chest hurts from trying to catch my breath. "Send another team to the skin zone. A kid told us someone is in there."

The sound of an order going out makes me sink onto the stairs in relief. We are still far enough ahead of the team who met us outside the maintenance hatch where I can relax. I only hope Wade is closer than Graham and Carson are, since Carl sits beside me.

"Man, we gotta stop finding charity cases this way," he says. "It's no good for the heart."

He has a point. While we make our spending creds finding lost stuff, we always manage to trip over major disasters. This time, it looks like Canoples is about to be the center of the next scandal.

Hoppin' space rocks! Where do they find the jerks making Security look bad?

I have a very good reason for hating anyone in Security who makes law enforcement look bad. As far as I'm concerned, anyone who breaks the law can spend the rest of their lives on Fomalhaut, the prison barge orbiting the Milky Way.

"Can you tell us where your mommy and daddy went?" I ask.

Might as well narrow down the area where the kid last saw her parents. I would have liked to ask her name, but I figure she won't tell anyone until someone uses the safe word.

I hope Chief Pelham recognizes her from the recent arrivals.

How do I know she belongs on Canoples Station? Well, I can say I'm psychic, but that sounds dumb. Or I can point at the locator beacon attached to her arm.

Every station has a code number for voice communication. Security engraves the same number in red on the black locater bands. I am looking at 10-8 on the girl's, the one for my home station. It is as plain as the nose on my face that she lives here, but I have never seen her before.

There are not that many kids on the station, only enough to set aside one level for the schools, just forty rooms. With ten kids per room, I have a very good chance of knowing a three-year-old like this one, especially since my mom works in the hospital's pediatric section.

Unlike those places on Earth, folks on the Twelve Stations visit the hospital for routine appointments. It makes for more space, a dreamed of luxury in our cramped quarters. And it makes more sense. Who wants to see a doctor in one place and then go to another area because he or she has to treat you in a controlled environment? That sounds more dangerous than a meteor storm during a flitter trip.

"BD help me find Mommy and Daddy?" The child squirms free of Carl and settles in my lap. "You always find things."

Nice to know my reputation has found a place in her brain, but she has something wrong. I tolerate small kids, in miniscule doses. Anymore, and I go insane.

"Security will find your parents," I say and check out the stairs, both up and down.

No one in sight yet. Just where are the chief and Wade? Are they stopping for a caf break? Has someone pulled a fresh batch of Venus-muts from the fryer? What is going on? Better yet, will someone bring me something to fill the massive hole opening in my stomach? Rescuing kids in trouble always makes me hungry. Passing out looms in my future unless I eat soon.

CHAPTER NINE

Minutes stretch until it feels like we have been sitting on the stairs for hours. The little girl curls up in my lap and presses every inch of her shaking body against my stomach in a tight ball. Hiccupy breaths and liquid splashing on my hand tells me she has started crying again, but the quiet kind kids do when they're scared out of their minds. That drives me nuts.

"You have that look on your face," Carl says.

"What look?" Like I have to ask.

"The one that says we're about to take on another charity case."

"Not happening." I rock back and forth in an effort to calm the kid. "Where's Pelham?"

I have about had it waiting for Security to show up, but only the ones I trust. Carl's face reflects the same frustration running through me.

"The ones below us will get here first," he says.

"I hear them."

Boy, can I hear those boots pounding on the steps. The ones above us move in a broken rhythm. Below us, they sound like a measured cadence, and there are a lot more than the number of men I saw earlier.

Ridiculous comes nowhere close to describing our situation. We have to get out of here, or at least go up some more. I set the kid on the step between Carl and me, and then I grab the railing and try to stand. Big emphasis on try. My legs cramp up tighter than a scientist's heart when Io's volcano burps. Despite the pain, I manage to stand upright and make an important discovery. I cannot take a step. It hurts too much.

"Man, this isn't good," Carl says. "Where's Pelham?"

Terry thuds down the stairs first, followed by Wade and Chief Pelham. Right in time, too. Graham and Carson come up the stairs below us at a dead run with at least a dozen men and women behind them, twice as many as those jerks had with them when we exited the skin zone. How many people does it take to catch two teens and a three-year-old?

One good thing happens. Graham, Carson, and their crew skid to a halt when they see their boss frowning at them.

"Bad men!" the girl screeches. "They hurt Mommy and Daddy."

Talk about dropping a furred up re-kat into the mess. Chief Pelham moves between her and his men. The kid literally climbs my leg until she clings to my neck. I sigh. This is not going to turn out well.

"Cantu-bean," Chief Pelham says. "Missy, where are your parents?"

Cantu-bean!?!?!?! *Yuck!* What are Missy's parents thinking? Not only do cantu-beans taste like a flitter's oil pan, a century after it needs an oil change, they stink like no other stench in the galaxy! No one will ever guess a safe word like that.

Hmmm … maybe cantu-bean is a great safe word.

"Unca John!" Missy flings herself at the chief. He catches her and holds her with one arm. "I waited and waited and waited for you to come. But you never did." She peeks at me. "But he did. I 'member what you say about BD Bradford. He okay to go with. But he take very, very, very." She takes a deep breath. "Very long time to come. And I can't make Mommy and Daddy wake up. And–"

"Okay," Chief Pelham says. "I get the idea."

"Uncle John?" I raise an eyebrow. "You told a little kid about me?"

Like I need any more fans, especially those less than two feet tall. An image of hundreds of Missy's trying to strangle me while I run for my life is too ugly to contemplate. Yet, the picture forms in my head.

Yuck!

"I warned her parents about you. She happened to be there." He smiles. "Now, Missy. Where are your parents?"

Before she has a chance to say anything else, the women who showed up with Graham walk away from him.

"You called for support capturing three fugitives," one says. "But we're chasing Bradford, Wills, and a baby. A baby." Her voice rises. "I can understand Bradford and Wills. Those two and Ashley piss me off sometimes. But a baby? You actually called a baby a fugitive? Get a psych check, Graham!"

She and the other women take off down the stairs at a run. Graham's face turns an even deeper shade of purple. Missy points at him.

"Bad men hurt Mommy and Daddy," she lisps. "They make us go with them when Mommy and me meet Daddy at safe place. The bad men hit Mommy and Daddy. They try to hit me, but I hide."

Graham, Carson, and their crew actually manage to look defiant. I'm sure they'll come up with a reasonable explanation for her accusation, probably going so far as to accuse her of lying. Problem is most three-year-olds can't lie. They just blurt out everything they hear and see.

"Where did you find her, BD?" Chief Pelham asks.

"About five hundred feet from the door to Stairwell Three inside the skin zone," I say.

No use holding back. Now is not the time to worry about the Asteroids game. I silently say goodbye to the trip I planned to Games and Vids. If I'm very lucky, what I earned earlier will cover the fine for going out of bounds.

Bye, bye Asteroids. No matter what I do or say, I will lose everything Governor Jackson gave us. I just can't do anything right today. And it's only ten!

"We heard her when we found Mrs. Jackson's travel bag," I say. "Carl and Terry didn't notify you because I wanted to return the property first."

There. I confessed. I still feel lousy. What will it take to change that? Do I have to tell everyone about the triple fee, to admit I thought about creds before a lost child? I'm a teen, supposedly kept around to irritate everyone, not a trained Security officer. So, why has the guilt just deepened inside me?

"Of all the selfish things you've ever done, this is the worst." Wade's explosive bellow is only a little lower than what I can expect from Mom. "Why didn't you call us right away?"

The jerks and their followers smirk. One of them at the back whispers what sounds like it's about time someone stopped me from doing what I want. Wade glares hard. I squirm while imagining how he will tell Mom that I put creds before a lost child. Only Chief Pelham doesn't seem upset, but he doesn't look happy either.

"Wade, take a recovery team into the skin zone," Chief Pelham says. "BD, spin me the tale from the beginning."

Sure sounds like he has no plans to believe me. I wait for Wade to take off before telling the story.

"But Chief," I say after explaining what we were doing in a forbidden area. "I wasn't sure someone said something. I could barely see the locater beacon. And I was hanging upside down." I shrug. "Well, I was sort of hanging. I'd just slipped. Carl and Terry were pulling me up when I saw her."

As best as I can, I put on my everybody-hates-me expression. I will do whatever it takes to make him believe me, even … I gag at the thought … grovel.

"That sounds too strange to be fiction." He blows out a frustrated breath. "You and your situations. I fully expect you to drag a Jupiter Man-Monster into my office one of these days."

Now, who needs a psych check? Everyone knows Jupiter Man-Monsters are a myth. And a lousy one at that.

"He help me." Missy bobs her head up and down. "No one else come when I cry. BD Bradford find me."

"He sure did." Terry snickers. "Is this another charity case?"

"It's not a charity case." I glare at him and Carl. "Wade will find her parents. It's a one time thing."

Sure. Do I really believe that? *Not.* Things just don't work out that well for me. No matter what I do, I always end up in the worst situation at a time when I have other plans. Shoving past Carson and Graham, I open the door to level fifteen.

"Coming?" I glance at my pals. "Or are you going to hang out with Security?"

"I'll stop by later," the chief says. "We need to talk."

Oh, just freakin' great. What else can go wrong? Whoa! I didn't just think something so outrageous. Did I?

Rats! I sure did.

Deep trouble looms for me. No matter what I want to happen, from this point until midnight, I'll live under a curse. How to turn the curse around eludes me.

Without waiting for the rest of my team, I race to another stairwell and run up it to level eight where our office is. There I can forget all about the humiliating experience.

I have to walk past the duo-flex doors outside Security to find safety. That means putting up with comments from the men and women hanging around instead of patrolling the station or giving teens a hard time.

Nah. They already have a great target for their humor. Me, and those bored officers fire their best shots. Too bad for them I decide words cannot hurt me. But a few do. I really don't suck Venus fumes.

Gross!

I slam into our tiny office. My heart takes off at high speed, thud-thud-thudding against my chest.

Someone stands right in front of me. No good reason exists for that person to have breached a locked door and wait in the dark. I gulp.

Clad in the same silvery jumpsuit I wear, the most beautiful gal in the galaxy looks up from my PerSys and frowns.

"What case did you open without asking me?"

Oh, that beautiful voice is directed at me. Can this day get any better? Well, it can. If the gal would just sweeten her question a little. And stop glaring at me like I'm the worst jerk in the galaxy.

CHAPTER TEN

The vision in front of me has to be a dream. Her very presence sucks the air out of an office so small one person is a crowd.

"Oh, please," she says. "Quit with the goopy expression. It's disgusting!"

The knife of indifference cuts deep, and she wields it so well. I think about losing the creds to get rid of the goopy expression, whatever that is. Somehow, with her in front of me, nothing gets me down.

She doesn't move. That makes me wonder. Is this the best dream I've had in months?

Only one thing can differentiate between a dream and possible glorious real life. I sniff, a long, deep one. The sweet smell of fresh flowers, an herbal cleanser she loves, fills my nostrils. No dream, real life has returned to me.

All my unspoken wishes have come true. Hope she wants to reclaim her spot as our number one investigator rises. Until her eyes tighten into a squint, and makes the glare directed at me even worse.

Oh, the pain those glares give me. No one knows, and I will never tell them, but my most fervent wish is for her to forgive me without me having to say the words "I'm sorry."

"Where were you?" she asks. "I've been here for hours! It's not like I have all day to hang around waiting for you."

Cassie Wills comes around the desk and thumps a finger against my chest. She can do that until I die of embarrassment as far as I'm concerned.

What can I say about her that others miss? For one thing, she isn't identical to Carl, like everyone else claims. She is five inches shorter than he is, and her blonde hair has really cool brown streaks in it. Not fake, like some of the girls did to prove they love Jenna Rock, the latest space-grunge/rap singer. Cassie's hair is completely natural, just like she is.

Now, I have to admit I could have held back my laughter when she made her big announcement. Making a crack about cheerleading being a girl thing is probably not one of my best moments.

Trouble is I believe she's one of the gang. She has never gone for girly stuff. If we have a case requiring us to crawl through the greasy tubes off the SpaceDock, she volunteers to go first and argues when we suggest she stay in the lounge. Her idea of fun is a pick-up game of SpaceBall on the same team as me. Together, we are unstoppable – until I blew it.

"Quit grinning at me," she snaps, dragging me back from daydreams of her resuming our former activities like nothing ever happened. "Tell me about this case. Why did you open it?"

"What case?" I slide around her by half sitting on Carl's desk and plop in front of the PerSys. "I've been working a case all morning, but I didn't enter it yet."

"Where's my cut?"

My temper rises. Not a good thing since I want her to understand I made a mistake, even if she was the one who abandoned us, to hang with her girlfriends and play at cheerleading. Where does she get off asking for a cut when she hasn't done a bit of work?

"Didn't see you hanging upside down off a girder to grab a travel bag with contraband in it," I say.

"No one told me," she says.

Oh yeah.

We never told her about the case, but it still doesn't make it right for her to ask for a cut. My hand goes to my pocket, where I have the creds Governor Jackson gave me.

Don't do it. Make her beg. My fingers gather up part of the creds. Hey, you, Bradford, she gave up on you.

Before I realize it, I hand over one hundred fifty creds, which leaves me sixty short to buy the longed for game.

Now, that's love. Right?

"Thanks." She pockets the creds. "Can you close out this case so I can take my name off the business? I have plans this afternoon."

Oh, thanks and close out a case I know nothing about so she can have fun. Who does she think she is? Better yet, who is this jerk inhabiting my body? Someone pinch me, tell me I have not just given away the creds I nearly cracked my head earning, in addition to having trouble with Security for failing to report seeing a locator beacon right away.

"What's the case?" I ask instead.

"Don't you know?" She flips a hand at a PerSys. "Some guy wants you to help him."

Curiosity kills the re-kat, but for BD Bradford, intrepid investigator, it activates the brain cells. I look for the case.

What?!?!?!?! Automatic case activation? How? Why? I move my gaze to the top of the message. Hoppin' space rocks!

My blood runs cold.

"Do me a favor." I open the properties to find out where the i-mail originated. "Get a hold of Carl and Terry. They're probably in Security. Tell them to get back here now. This is huge."

That's the understatement of the century. I finish speaking; saying another word is as impossible as spacewalking without protective gear. My danger radar flicks into high gear. Alarms scream inside my head.

The i-mail originates from an inactive account; one used by my dad before his disappearance.

This is dead wrong. No way. Not a word for five years, and now an anonymous message arrives at my business with someone else's name as the sender. What is going on?

"I'm not your messenger." She jams a finger against the door's actuator. "Call Carl and Terry yourself. Then get that case closed so I can take my name off this crummy business."

"Please, Cassie?" I beg. "It's not like I asked you to work a case.

And I did give you half of my cut."

Oops. Leaving out the last part might have sounded – what's that word – sensitive. Yeah … sensitive.

"You're the most insensitive jerk in the galaxy," she says.

The pain in her voice slashes through me so much that I can't express an objection. I'm not a jerk. There is a little sensitivity in me, in my pinky finger.

I look up in time to see her back as she runs off.

"What I said wasn't all that bad. Was it?"

Even if someone gives me a vid-book to teach me about girls, I still won't understand them. They're too weird.

Now that she's gone, my ability to think straight returns. She always does that to me. I figure she always will, but I blew it with her. Cassie will never come near me again.

Since she pretty much told me to make my own calls, I fish my PocketPad from my jumpsuit and call Carl. Ten rings and no answer. Strange. His PocketPad is on, but he hasn't picked up nor has he activated the message function. I try Terry with the same response.

"Where are you guys?"

Frustrated, both by the message, and my friends' non-response, I transfer the mysterious i-mail to my PocketPad's files section and go into the corridor. After securing the door, I wander over to Security. The same group of officers still stands at the reception desk. They look like they're waiting for the Venus-mut cart to deliver.

From what I know about Earth, Venus-muts are a lot like

doughnuts. Made of sweetened dough, they spend some time in a deep fat fryer. There the resemblance ends. What has everyone on the Twelve Stations fighting over the treats are the toppings. Great, fresh fruit with nuts all over the sauce.

Yummy. Certainly takes care of what Mom called my bottomless pit – three dozen at a time.

Since there is no sign of the fresh treat, I take care of pressing business by going into Security.

"Seen Carl or Terry?" I ask.

The silence greeting me makes me feel like I have a case of space-flu, a little problem that comes around every year about the time school lets out for Long Break, what kids on Earth thought of as their summer vacation. The virus keeps a lot of kids stuck in a hospital bed instead of enjoying their vacation. Scientists claim the source of space-flu eludes them, making it impossible to eradicate the disease. Me? I've always believed it's some parent's way of making sure their kid doesn't spend too much time on the promenade – kind of like allowance control.

"You talking about your partners?" One of the officers, Billy Small, asks.

"Well, I'm not talking about your space hooch dreams," I retort.

Wrong person to talk to about space hooch dreams. He nearly lost his life when a couple of guys drunk out of their minds on the homemade booze crashed into the SpaceDock. He escaped by diving under a counter, right into the arms of an old lady. She thought he was the best thing to come along since the evacuation of Earth. Poor Small has spent the last two years avoiding her efforts to marry him to her granddaughter.

"Stairwell?" I ask.

"Nah." He grins, one promising retribution at a later, unspecified date. "Skin zone off sub-three. The chief said you know where the spot is, so we're to tell you to hoof it back there as soon as we see you."

"Yeah. Right. Whatever."

No way will I let him see the idea of returning to the place where I almost ended up spaced bothers me. Sauntering over to the door, I make my way back inside the stairwell before leaning against a wall to let my heart slow down.

I can say it's an aftereffect of Cassie being in the office, or running up all those stairs earlier, but that's not the truth. Like every other space dweller, spacing scares me. There is no recovery from it. To return to the place where it almost happened, less than an hour later, brings my fear to a level I have never experienced.

"Ah, no one will start a sweep with Chief Pelham inside the skin zone."

I hope.

After taking my time getting to the skin zone, I expect to find no one but my buds and the chief. *Boy, am I wrong. That makes it twice in one day.* I wonder, as I sidle toward Carl and Terry, if what I want to do about the message will be number three.

CHAPTER ELEVEN

Reaching my buds proves harder than I first figured. The access hatch brings the first obstacle, in the form of my old nemesis, Graham. He stares at me. I saunter over to where he stands at the entrance. A smile settles on his face as his thick arm flies up to block my path, at the same level as my face.

"Ready to upset your boss again?" I ask. "Chief Pelham wants to see me. You're in my way."

"Ready to admit you messed up?" he asks.

Arms folded across my chest, I tap a foot while shooting him *the glare*, my patented expression to shame adults into backing off.

It wasn't my fault. Too many people failed to make sure no one was in the skin zone before the sweep activated.

One person knew someone might be in danger. Me, and that makes part of this situation my fault. Carl, Terry, and I have to take some of the blame because we did what we always do, rush into action without thinking.

Darn! The back of my jumpsuit's sticking to me. Thanks, Cassie. Two minutes around you, and I'm acting like a fool. Again!

My usual reaction around her, but not anyone or anything else, almost makes me back off. Before I do, Graham lowers his arm. I take off butt stop fast when another officer blocks my path. Some fast-talking gets me past him, but there are a lot more nasty green uniforms between me and the guys.

"Chief Pelham wants to see me," I insist the twentieth time a Security officer stops me. "Call him."

"He's busy. Wait for him in the corridor." The woman turns her back on me. "Thanks to you and your nosy pals, we have to grub around in this mess. What a waste."

What else does she have to do? If she hates grubbing around, she can find another job. As soon as she starts going through a pile of junk, I look for Terry and Carl again and find them in an area that seems familiar. *Too familiar.* I check the piles Missy reached for during our escape earlier, but they're no longer around. The trash is now all over the place. Two groups of medics work feverishly where the junk once sat.

My heart drops into my boots. We made a terrible mistake. *A horrible mistake.* Me and my buds might be partly responsible for someone's ... death. The nastiest, ugliest feeling in the galaxy fills me. My dad died on patrol, but nothing I could have done would have prevented it. A few older folks died in the last few years, but theirs was a normal end of life. Carl, Terry, and I have never done anything this bad. Ever.

"This stinks," I mutter. "Why didn't I check out those junk piles? The sweep had already stopped."

Terry and Carl ignore me when I join them. Their horrified gazes remain locked on the medics treating a man and a woman. From Missy's hysterical sobs, I figure they must be her parents.

"There are green lights on the stretchers," I say, referring to the built-in diagnostic systems.

"Still not good," Carl answers. "Neither has responded to any resuscitation effort."

"Why?"

My question goes unanswered. I wish I stayed with the guys instead of letting my temper get the better of me. Or went after Cassie to get my creds back. The idea of public humiliation from her is a lot better than listening to a three-year-old cry.

"Want Mommy and Daddy," Missy wails, cranking up my guilt even more. "Please help them, Unca John. Make Mommy and Daddy wake up."

Listening to her heartbroken plea drives home one thing. My own wants seem very selfish. Big deal about giving up creds for Asteroid. Me and the guys have pooled our resources in the past when we ran short. So what if we have to hang together when playing or take turns?

Please, someone, take away this load of guilt.

"Why is Missy here?" I ask. "I thought Wade took her to the hospital."

"No one could find her parents," Terry says.

"I tried, but this place looks different with the lights on." Carl looks at me with anguish written all over his face. "Chief Pelham had

Wade bring Missy back. She went right to her parents." His eyes tighten when the little girl wails even louder. "I never want to witness anything like this again."

Neither do I, and I missed the moment. Of course, catching this part of the experience sets my brain into overdrive, to find a reason to leave. The mysterious message burns through me, and demands that I deal with it now.

"Guys, we have to get out of here," I say. "We have a big problem."

"Did Cassie burn your ears?" Carl asks.

"Nah," Terry says. "She probably made him trip over his feet. Give up, BD. Apologize. Grovel. She'll forgive you." He wobbles a hand back and forth. "About the time the sun goes nova."

Such good friends. Do they even have a clue about reality?

It sure isn't a couple fighting for their lives. While I care what happens to Missy, I can't let her problem divert me from the explosive message.

"Look at this." I open the message and thrust my PocketPad in front of Terry's face.

He reaches up to push the device away, but then he grabs it.

"Where did this message come from?" he asks. "When did we receive it? Pluto gas! Did you erase the original? I can't trace a message unless we still have it."

Ugh, can't Terry come up with another way of showing his disgust?

Pluto gas was once harvested from the small planet, in order to run some of the food processing plants. That lasted for about three seconds, when the smell drove everyone out of the factory near the planet.

"What's it all about?" Carl peaks at the message. "Is this person for real? No one disappears for five years without a trace and then pops up with a message like this."

"Got that straight," Terry agrees.

I press between them to read the message again. The three sentences reignite hope my dad is still around.

Pirate threat. Need assist. Notify Security. Jameson.

Eric Jameson had been Dad's second-in-command the day his flitter disappeared. When Carson and Graham came back with the laser-streaked pieces, they claimed they found no sign of the crew. No one else has ever lucked onto answers to the biggest mystery in the galaxy. Has someone finally given me what I need to find my dad? If so, what will it take to figure out where Jameson is, and how fast I can get in touch with him?

"We have to tell Chief Pelham," Carl whispers. "Did Cass see this?"

Only he gets away with shortening her name. I used to, until I made an idiot of myself.

"Why?" Terry asks. "All we have is a message we can't trace, unless BD didn't erase the original. What good will that do?"

"The original is still on my PerSys," I say. "Cassie did see it, when she came to the office to take her name off the business. So, ask me the next question. I'm sure you'll like the answer."

"Where did it originate?" Carl asks.

"Right here." I point at the access door. "On Sub-three."

Their astounded expressions match the emotions running through me. Sub-three is the station's storage area. In a world where space is a precious commodity, we give up one level on each station to store goods no longer needed but still in great shape. When someone relocates here, they pick out what they need.

Sub-three has one other function because of double plating. During emergencies, everyone evacuates to shelters on the other side of the level until it's safe.

"We need Cass," Carl says. "She's the only one who can figure this out."

"What about Terry?" I demand. "Cassie's not the only one who can figure out where this message originated. 'Cause, let me tell you, it sure wasn't Sub-three. There aren't any working computers down here unless this person carried it in. According to the header, it was done on an OfficeSys." I glance at the message header again. "And, man, that's one old program. Ancient tech. Who uses version 2.0 anymore? We're at 12.8 for i-mails!"

A thought runs through my mind, but I quickly discard it as outrageous. There are too many safeguards on the stuff jammed into the many storage units down here. How would this person have hooked a PerSys up to the station's power grid and intranet provider?

Nothing about this situation makes sense.

"We have to talk to Chief Pelham." I swallow a large lump in my throat. If Jameson survived, there is a very good chance my dad is out there somewhere. "Maybe Dad's a hostage. Someone might have used him to access sensitive areas of the station. Maybe he finally found a way to tell us about it."

Now I'm acting dumb. Dad would have known, and anyone else with half a brain, the codes changed the second Chief Pelham heard the report about the flitter's destruction. But I have to believe something. It's not like my dad to disappear without an explanation, so I've always wondered if someone caused the accident. Without a body, I tell people I accepted his death, but it's the biggest lie I ever told.

"Don't go there," Terry says. "I checked out the wreckage. This is a hoax, BD."

"Maybe it's not." I stroke the message.

The screen blurs for a second before the images reform. Jameson escaped pirates to send a message. Someone on Canoples knows about him. No one sneaks onto a station. Sure, we have a lot of access hatches, but radar and constant patrols in addition to vid-cameras ensure Security knows what's going on at all times. Only one reason exists for me and the guys never trying to sneak in through one of the exterior hatches, and it's not because no one else has ever done it. We can't figure out how to get past all the backup systems to disable anything that might record our actions.

"Why didn't they bring Jameson to Security?" I whisper. "Why didn't the message say anything about my dad? What's going on?"

"Call Cassie," Terry says. "This is way beyond what I can do. We need answers, and the way we need to get them involves things I haven't even begun to play with yet."

Carl pulls out his PocketPad. I take mine back and turn toward Chief Pelham.

"Just be sure you tell Cassie asking for her help wasn't my idea," I say over a shoulder. "She sure doesn't want anything to do with me."

That's my biggest problem. She makes me feel funny inside. The guys think the whole situation is hysterical. All I want is to figure out what she has done to me and fix it … if I can.

CHAPTER TWELVE

Carl begs during most of his conversation with Cassie. Nothing he says makes me feel good about her coming back. I try to tune out the humiliating exchange by searching the area for clues. Not much luck with that. What Security hasn't already gathered as evidence looks like a recycler's reject.

"Come on, Cass," he says. "Just this one case, sis. It's really important. More important than hanging around the promenade."

He turns around, grinning and holding up a thumb. Terry glances at me and mouths one. I mouth back two and three. Right at that second, Carl winces and yanks the PocketPad from his ear.

"Sorry, Cass," he says. "I didn't mean your plans aren't important, but this is really huge. I can't tell you what it is unless you agree to help 'cause it's super-secret."

I learn a few things about groveling from him. No one will ever catch me doing it!

"I'll be right back," I say to Terry.

Unwilling to listen to anymore of Carl's pleas, I walk over to where Chief Pelham stands with Wade and Missy. To get to them, I have to pass the medics. As soon as I see bruises and dried blood on the injured couple, my conscience kicks me in the butt. She tried to point out where her parents were, but I refused to pay attention to her silent plea. We had already stopped the sweep. We put more importance on making creds, and now she has to witness this.

While I kick myself mentally, I stop beside the man I need to talk to. Chief Pelham looks at me and then back at the couple on the stretchers. The medics have finally stabilized them and are setting up for transport. Sure doesn't make sense to me, on a space station with all the latest state-of-the-art medical equipment, they carry the emergency stretchers by hand to the hospital on level twelve, far above us.

Usually, when Security locates someone who has been in danger of spacing, they request a doctor come along with the med techs, but one isn't around today. Everything is a huge mess, and I can't figure out why.

"What's up?" Chief Pelham asks when I snort.

"Kind of need to talk to you without Missy around," I say and smile at the little girl. "How do you know her?"

He shifts her to his other shoulder. Missy sticks a thumb into her mouth and closes her eyes.

"Her dad and I went to Brachin Academy near Mars back when we were a couple of terroristic teens." He chuckles. "Kind of hard to imagine now, isn't it?"

Boy, is that the truth. John Pelham embodies Security Chief. All people have to do is look at him, and they know what he does. It's the hardness in his eyes, and the way he holds himself more than anything. I sure know I don't want him coming after me if I ever think about breaking the law.

"You don't need to say anything. Bud Williams and I reformed our ways a long time ago," he says. "So, what has Canoples Investigations upset today?"

"We have a new case." I glance at Carl and Terry. They are busy talking on a PocketPad. "This one is weird. I don't think we can handle it." *Without Cassie, and she sure won't help after she finds out what it's about.* "The case activated itself when a message came in on our office PerSys."

"You need better firewalls," he says. "Are you sure the message wasn't meant for Security?"

Yeah his office is right next to mine. Someone might have mixed up the addresses.

Not!

No one with half a brain can mix up canoplessecurity@canoples.gov with canoplesinvestigations@canoples.biz. It just isn't possible.

"The message had three sentences," I say, ignoring his comment. "But I don't want anyone else to know." I lower my voice to a whisper. "It's from Jameson."

Chief Pelham jerks his head at Wade. My big brother strolls over and takes the time to smooth imaginary wrinkles out of his already perfect uniform on the way.

"Take Missy to the hospital, and have Angela check her out," the chief says. "Then stay with Bud and Cindy until they come around and get their statements." He glances at me. "BD and I have to talk about something important. It's ears only. He'll only tell someone I've pre-approved to hear about it, so don't question him at home."

"Yes, sir." Wade lifts Missy from the chief's shoulder. The child curls up against his arm and coos. "I'll get right on it."

Scorching hot steam looms in my future, but laughter bursts out of me no matter how hard I try to hold it back. Wade once told me he hates kids.

Sure looks like a kid has taken to him.

"Real mature," he says in a scornful voice. "Soothing an upset child is part of my training. She's only responding to my non-vocal movements."

Like huh? Does he really think I'll let him off so easily?

"They still have to trust you," I say around sputters. "This one acts like you're her … her … *Dad*!"

His face goes eggplant purple. He's always maintained he never wants kids after helping Mom raise me after Dad's death.

"Oh, grow up," Wade growls.

After the medical transport takes off with him escorting them, Chief Pelham holds out a hand.

"Let me see the message," he says.

"Sure." I hand over my PocketPad. "I can tell you what it says, and where it came from."

"How do you know?" He sighs. "Never mind. I might have to fine you if you tell me." He reads the message and shakes his head. "I can see where your overactive imagination went after reading this. BD, there's no chance Tom survived this long without letting someone know he was alive."

"Isn't there?" ask. "Dad would take his time to make sure no one traced his path. You know that."

"Yeah. I do."

"So why isn't it possible Dad survived? What if it's true? You said yourself there were pirates operating in one of the nebulas between here and Uranus. We need to track this down." I glance at my buds. "We traced the source to Sub-Three, but we're stuck. Cassie can do better, but she's kind of torqued at me."

"The whole station knows that." Chief Pelham laughs. "So far, you've blown three pools on when she'll crucify you on the promenade. I lost fifty creds yesterday."

"Gee, thanks," I retort. "Have a little faith. I figured out why I upset her, but she won't give me a chance."

"Grovel. It always works for me. Make up with Cassie." He drops a hand onto my shoulder. "I'm letting Canoples Investigations run with this because I have a few problems in Security. The four of you will report to me only. No one else, not even Wade. Don't talk about this where anyone else can hear you. Do you understand?" He lowers his head to examine the debris littered floor. "Bud works for Internal Security. I asked him to come here because I suspect some of my people are working for smugglers or maybe pirates."

Understand him? My biggest problem is have I heard Chief Pelham right? After a couple of seconds, when no one tells me my hearing is wonky, I nod and take off to join Carl and Terry. We have a lot of work to do. The biggest problem is finding a way to let Cassie humiliate me. I hope I survive the encounter.

It hits me like a ton of space rocks. Survival is in my future, if a few things work in my favor. Unless, of course, Cassie decides it's time to get even.

Would she really do that? Oh yeah, and a few other things to make me the target of a lot of teasing. I can always hope for a quiet moment for us to get past our differences.

Fat chance!

CHAPTER THIRTEEN

While walking over to Carl and Terry, I close the mysterious message and turn off my PocketPad. Mom might yell later, but I have no worries. One thing works in my favor. Missy will no doubt keep Mom busy for hours. Terry and Carl look up when I stop in front of them.

"We really messed up. Big time," Carl mutters. "We should have reported that locator beacon right away."

"How much trouble are we in?" Terry asks and gulps. "My dad will make me go to work with him if the chief calls one more time."

The thought of having my team split up hurts, but it might happen. We are in more trouble than we ever have been in the past, but I know something the guys don't, and I can't share right now.

"Later," I whisper.

Wade strides past with Missy sleeping against his shoulder. He stops before we have a chance to get away. The look on his face tells me I'm in for a hard time, and he gives me a hard time about the stupidest stuff. Things like cleaning my room and showing up for meals when Mom wants me to aren't as important as my current case. The second he tracks me down after I blow off her rules, he stares at me until I return home and take care of the problem.

He's my big brother, not my dad. I remind him about that every single time he treats me like a little kid, but he refuses to listen.

"What were you thinking?" Wade asks. "Or were you thinking?"

The desire to sink through the deck to avoid his scolding is almost overwhelming, but I decide a head-on attack has a chance of avoiding the humiliating tongue-lashing he's about to unleash.

"Why are you still here? Don't you have to protect the kid?" I ask.

Missy hiccups in her sleep. Guilt creeps through me at how uncaring I sound. In the space of less than an hour, she has crawled past my defenses until I want to protect her.

"I had to speak to the chief," Wade says. "Not that it's any of your business."

"You're sticking your nose in my business," I say.

"Mom will flip when she hears about today," he says.

"Don't tell her," I suggest.

I want to remind him he's not my shadow, but dare not. No matter how well I explain, Mom always takes Wade's side whenever we disagree.

"You know I can't do that." He rubs Missy's back when she wiggles. "Look at her. Imagine, if you can, how scared she felt when your selfish actions made her stay down here almost an hour longer than she had to. Then figure out how to explain your greed to Missy."

He never once raises his voice, which makes every word feel like gravity loss slamming me into a wall. I glance at Terry and Carl.

Shoulders slumped; they fasten their gazes on the deck. They look as lousy as I feel, but Wade won't get away with humiliating us.

"Don't you think we know we messed up? We're almost adults. Almost." I hold up a finger when he opens his mouth. "We get to make mistakes. This was a big one. We already figured that out. Quit beating us up over it."

With a quick glance, he looks me up and down. I see a glimmer of what looks like grudging respect in his eyes.

"Maybe you are growing up." He jerks his head in a short, sharp nod. "Don't let anything like this happen again."

He leaves, and I blow out a relieved breath. Wade might not have said the words, but I know, without any doubts, he won't report my stupidity to Mom. *This time.* I'm sure if I repeat my mistake, she'll know every detail.

"We need to jet." I look around to make sure none of the Security officers hanging around us are listening and then lower my voice. "Chief Pelham wants us to track down the source of the you-know-what, and," I gulp back complete, total, utter fear. "We have to convince Cassie to help us." Sweat breaks out on my forehead. "In public. Where is she?"

Carl snorts with laughter. "On the promenade." He grins, the most evil one I have ever seen him do. "With Lisa."

My luck, never good when it comes to Cassie, throws me a wild card I never expected. Not finding her with Lisa is one of the things I counted on after my girl called me a jerk.

"Let's get it over with." I walk toward a lift.

My buds and me usually avoid lifts like they carry a space-flu epidemic. Lifts are for old folks, not guys in their prime. Today, with Chief Pelham counting on me to track down the source of the message, I have to obey the rule about not using the stairs to go to other levels.

"My best chance of figuring out where the message came from is down here," Terry says. "I can hang back and meet you later."

"Believe me, you want to see this," I snap. "Everyone will. Carl, why don't you send out a message to every kid on the station so they don't have to hear about it later? You're about to witness me groveling."

They roar with laughter while I stab the lift button. No way am I looking forward to what will be the most humiliating moment in my life since Dad disappeared, but I have no choice.

Well, a choice does exist, but Canoples Investigations never gives up on a case. We always find a way to solve whatever comes our way. With Cassie angry at me, I have to figure out if crawling over to her or just telling her how sorry I am until she relents will work.

"What did the chief tell you?" Carl asks after we're on our way.

"He gave us the case because he has problems," I say. "We can't talk about it where anyone can hear, so that pretty much leaves out the whole station except our office."

Oh yeah, the chief has problems. For him to rely on us, he must not trust very many of his people. Those he needs for other jobs, like cleaning up his ranks before everyone on the Twelve Stations knows.

"Someone could hear us in there, if they're in the room next to ours," Terry says.

"It's empty," I say, referring to the office beside ours. "Chief Pelham will probably make sure no one's in his office when we're in ours, so we can discuss the case." I look at my boots. "There's more."

"Does it have anything to do with you acting like an idiot around my sister?" Carl asks.

"Everything," I admit. "Chief Pelham won't let us keep the case unless she helps."

"How much memory do you have on your vid-cam?" Terry asks Carl. "I want pictures."

While they decide how much they can remotely unload to their PerSyses, I moan. My mind conjures up images of the entire station witnessing the culmination of the argument that began when I let Cassie know what I thought about her deviation from normal.

Did she blow off my comment like she always did in the past?

Oh no! That would have been too easy.

Cassie turned so red she looked like she just returned from a visit to Mistlich, near Venus, and their solar filters failed. Instead of explaining why I was wrong, she called me a Pluto-lover and took off.

Pluto-lovers are fools who want the Ruling Council to reinstate the icy rock as a planet. Way back when I was eight, the controversy surrounding Pluto came up during a meeting on Aldebbaran. The governors of the Twelve Stations called for a galaxy wide vote to settle everything once and for all. No big surprise as to the outcome, no one wanted responsibility for a planet there was no way to use for manufacturing or tourism.

That wasn't the end of the "Is Pluto a planet?" question. Every couple of years, a long distance shuttle stops for a few days, and those freaks wander all over the station, trying to convince people to join them.

Me, a Pluto-lover? Wrong!

I made my next mistake without thinking, and I still regret it. Right in the middle of the promenade, with most of the station eating lunch, I yelled at Cassie's back.

"I'd rather be a Pluto-lover than listen to you talk about girl stuff."

Then I laughed like her opinion meant nothing to me. Cassie never even looked at me. She walked over to Lisa and started whispering. The war between us escalated us at that second, but as I think about it, the whole thing makes no sense.

Lately, nothing makes sense, especially the message from Jameson. I watch the lights on the lift while approaching my doom. Visions flash before my eyes, but they have nothing to do with the case. Every single one of them relates to the mortifying scene I'm about to start, and I have no idea how I will put up with all the witnesses sure to be hanging out on the promenade.

A bell dings. Sweat slithers out of every pore. Carl and Terry's grins widen as they finish transferring pics. While the door opens, I wish Cassie was anywhere else.

To my horror, my fervent wish has not happened. The heart of the station bustles with activity. Everyone comes to the promenade to play games, snack at the many eating booths, and buy what they need. Stores of every kind sit between arcades and snack shacks.

"Looks busy." Terry grins at me.

Families move through groups of teens. Men and women talk to each other. Kids trade gaming tricks near a large tree in the center.

"Messages out," Carl announces. "But it sure looks like everyone's already here."

My gaze focuses on the tree, one of the few still left from the evacuation. When Earth's leaders ordered everyone off the dying planet, they also transplanted trees, flowers, fruits, and vegetables. Every station has a small greenhouse, some with artificial sunlight, and others dependent on the sun to make the food grow. An aspen grows on every promenade in the Twelve Stations. They aren't the original trees. Station life causes them to die after fifty years. This one is the sixth on Canoples Station. My granddad commemorated this particular tree, back when he was the governor.

At a table near the tree, I catch sight of the prettiest girl on the station. She sure is here. Seeing her sitting with Lisa makes me want to spew the lunch I have yet to eat, and do one other thing. Even though it's impossible, I want to travel back to the first tree's commemoration ceremony, when life was so much simpler. That will give me the chance to avoid certain embarrassment.

There is always the chance a more important case will begin right in front of our eyes, so I can avoid what I know is about to happen.

"There she is." Carl points at her.

"Order a Gut-Buster," I say. "I'll need it after I'm done."

The massive, overloaded pizza will help me forget the humiliating laughter after I grovel.

CHAPTER FOURTEEN

Cassie sits in the center of a bunch of brain-challenged girls. After tilting her head to one side to look at me like I'm a space slug, she squeals with laughter at something one of them says.

"I'm gonna spew," Carl says. "Let's jet, BD. Tell the chief we couldn't do it."

Lisa Tulane, all two hundred and fifty pounds of her, leans forward, and she gets closer to my girl. Cassie smiles at Lisa. Jealously rips through my guts. How can my girl even sit close to her? This is beyond believable. No one wants to be anywhere close to a monster like that.

Lisa stands all of five feet tall. Not exactly short, according to station standards, but she has to look up at most people over twelve. She has bright red hair and brown eyes. Green streaks in her hair and lavender implants circling her pupils makes her look like a space-ghoul, the legendary creatures haunting Mars.

The seams of her jumpsuit threaten to split. Even from this distance, I dread the experience. The visual in my head comes close to making me run for my life.

"This is gonna be great." Terry snaps pics. "We can use these on our website for advertising!"

That's an even worse visual. I can just imagine what kinds of cases we'll have if he follows through with his threat.

"It's up to you." I shrug, hoping my buds believe I don't care even though I do. "But you'll have every nut in the galaxy contacting us."

"Don't do it, Terry," Carl begs. "Our cases are weird enough already."

Cassie and Lisa hug each other and scream with more laughter at something Jake says. My hopes rise.

Say what? How can my hopes rise when the girl I love laughs with my sworn enemies?

Terry, Carl, and Cassie have hung out with me since we were two. We went to the same daycare. We attend school in the same classes every year. All of us came up with the idea for Canoples Investigations less than a day after my dad disappeared, hours before Carson and Graham came back from the shortest search in history. For the last couple of years, whenever anyone saw one of us, the others were close.

To say we know everything about each other comes nowhere close to true. During too many of what everyone calls our charity cases, we charge in without talking about what to do. Everything always turns out okay, until I acted like a dummy with Cassie. All this leads me to this micro-second, where I know when she's putting up with someone, and when she is really enjoying herself.

The laugh, the one that should have made me run for my life, alerts me to something very important. Cassie is having a miserable time. She's trying to prove how much fun she is having, but it isn't working.

"She sounds really jazzed." Carl elbows me. "Ready for this?"

No way will I let him know I've already figured out Cassie is tired of the adore-Lisa-Tulane-and-Jake-Tigley-Club. It's what we call the teens hanging around the table where Cassie sits. Jake leans against the protective fence surrounding the tree. He folds his arms across his chest and frowns when he sees me.

"BD's here," he announces at the top of his voice, sounding, as always, like a flitter engine about to explode. "His sidekicks are with him."

"Scary." Lisa screeches with laughter. "Run before he finds out we closed the Venus-mut stand."

Cassie stares at me, her eyes icy blue asteroids ready to crash through my defenses. Not much effort required on her part. I'm more sorry than I can ever tell her, but that's the impossible part. Apologies stick in my throat and doom me to her hatred forever.

Hoppin' space rocks! Can my day get any worse?

"Yeah." I roll my eyes. "Let's do it. The sooner Cassie comes to her senses the sooner we can finish this case."

Why do I feel like I just condemned myself to a fate worse than death? Must be the triumphant look on Jake's face. He leans over and whispers with Lisa. She grins.

"Oh, now we're really hot." I take off across the promenade at high speed. "Better make sure everyone's here. They won't want to miss this."

Did I mention I saw them around the tree? Well, it doesn't mean they're all that close. We have to walk from the far end of the promenade to the middle. Since Canoples Station is three miles across, we have quite a hike in front of us.

Carl and Terry prove their friendship by sending out message after message. Teens burst out of arcades and food stands to gather around Cassie and her group. She stands up and glares at me.

One thing is still the same.

I never slow my pace while pushing through the growing crowd. None other than Graham and Carson offer *me* advice.

"Try crawling. Worked with my girlfriend," Graham says.

Is he kidding? Does he really believe I'll ever take his advice? And a girlfriend?

Shiver and shudder. That image is far worse than the one of Lisa's jumpsuit ripping apart at the seams.

"Nah. Walk. Keep your head up. Don't let her see you upset," Carson says. "And do it today, Bradford, so I don't lose my bet."

It looks like just about everyone who hates me is around today. I even see Governor and Mrs. Jackson watching, but without Chuckles the re-kat.

Oh, just freakin' great! Those guys must have something better to do. Like catching kids making off with game chips, or an old guy taking an extra cup of caf.

Carson and Graham dog my footsteps as I approach my doom. *I guess not.* Cassie shoves through the crowd and stops me a good ten feet from them.

"I know why you're here." Her triumphant smile tells me I have to work for her cooperation. "It won't be easy."

"Is it ever?" I shrug and swallow a bunch of times to dislodge the apology. "I'm sorry, Cassie. It was just too funny to ignore. So, I'm a jerk. You've always known that."

Not the best way to apologize, but everyone who knows me also knows one other thing. I don't back off when I think I'm right. Never have. I can admit when I'm wrong, but I sure go out of my way to make it look like it's someone else's fault. Maybe I just figured out I love Cassie, but she won't have a chance to use that against me, and she can forget all about public humiliation.

A grin spreading across my face, I slam my fists against my hips and spread my legs. I'm no vid star, nor do I sing well. Mom says a re-kat with a stepped on tail sounds better. But I can and will make the most of my reputation as the number one private investigator on the station.

Strike station. I'm the best in the galaxy.

My cocky attitude wants to run, along with my feet, when she closes the space between us. For the second time during this too long day, we're close. If I want to, I can reach out and touch her. And I want to. More than I want food. More than I dread humiliation.

"Hey, Cassie," I say.

"You won't get away with it." She stabs a finger against my chest and hollers into my face. "Who do you think you are, BD Bradford? I'll tell you. You're a jerk. No way will I take your attitude anymore."

Cheers rise from Lisa's crowd. I grin and hold my ground. The cheering subsides, and everyone gets real quiet. My grin widens. Cassie and I always act like this when we both think we're right.

"Don't get up in my face," I shoot back at her. "You did something I never expected. How did you want me to react? Kiss your feet?"

Groans greet my announcement. Creds change hands. I chalk up a score for me and press my point.

"You conned me out of money I earned," I yell loud enough for everyone watching us to hear. "So, since you didn't work for it, it's time you showed up and did your job."

"Okay." She steps back.

Okay? Who is she kidding? Cassie Wills never gives up that easily.

CHAPTER FIFTEEN

People close to us pile creds into Carl's hands. Terry moves through the crowd and collects from everyone else. I look around in amazement. My buds, my best friends in the whole galaxy, bet against me.

No! Wait! They're collecting after it's clear I won. They bet on me.

They must have left the date open, since everyone else gave me a hard time about losing their money, and they thought they knew when Cassie and me would make up. The creds will come in handy while we turn down our usual work to deal with this case.

"We have to get to work." I move closer to her. "Make this good. 'Cause we can't tell you what it is until we get somewhere private."

"Gotcha." She smiles, the brightest, widest smile I have ever seen on her. "Do I get to crucify you?"

Who am I to blow her expectations? The intended target that has to live with the humiliation. No way will I go through that.

Tough luck if it upsets her. We have better things to do than put on a show.

"Nah." I shake my head. "Chief Pelham bet on yesterday. We're working for him now, so you can't rub it in."

"Okay."

To my amazement, she pecks my cheek and runs back to Lisa. After a fast conversation, where the leader of the two T's smacks the table, Cassie comes back.

"I am so glad I don't have to hang with Lisa anymore," she says. "She's a total loss."

Yes! I want to pump my fist in the air, but I settle for reaching for her hand. She twists her fingers around mine. Lisa stands and begins to waddle toward us. Her chins, both of them, quiver up and down. Tears glitter in her lavender edged brown eyes when Terry stops in front of her.

"Six thousand creds," he says. "The sun didn't go nova, Lisa."

"You're mean!" She sucks her lower lip between her teeth and turns around. "Daddy said I didn't have to pay. We're still kids, and we can't gamble."

She slides a foot backward and looks for an escape route. Carl darts over to cut off her escape.

"You signed a waiver." He holds up his PocketPad. "Pay up or –" He grins at the crowd. "You'll have everyone telling the rest of the station how you wiggled out of the pool when you lost."

Technically, she's right, but if she refuses to pay, no one will trust her again. She looks around. Everyone backs away.

"Meanie!" She squalls, but she gives Carl the creds.

Most teens carry a few hundred creds when hanging at the promenade, but Lisa never shows up with less than ten thousand, and she always leaves broke. From the tears now dripping down her face, her absence might happen a lot faster than normal today.

"Let's jet," I say. "I don't want to watch Lisa cry."

"Pathetic," Cassie says.

We walk toward the lifts.

"I have to tell Carl and Terry to meet us at the office," I say.

"They'll figure it out." She glances at me. "Is this about that message I saw?"

She is always right on the cred. Her short break hasn't dulled her deductive powers. With her beside me, we'll finish and hoof it back up to the promenade in no time.

Maybe we'll even have a chance to scope out Asteroids. I really want a chance at that game before everyone has played it.

"Yeah. We can't talk about it where someone can hear us." I check out the area.

Everyone is still busy giving up their creds. Relief runs through me. I'm not sure if Carl and Terry will share their winnings, but I have no plans to argue with them about it. This particular case will stretch all our skills past limits we have already stretched. A year might not give us enough time to figure it out.

Cassie and I keep walking. Our hands remain together. It's so easy to make up with her that I wonder why she held out for so long. The smell of flowers drifts around me; a smell I missed a lot while she and I were mad at each other. We slow as we approach the lift. I reach out with my free hand to press the actuator and think about the time we'll have alone.

The lift doors open before my fingers touch the actuator pad, and I stop thinking about anything, but the man stumbling out of the lift. As tall as me, he has a blank look on his face. Reddish-gold stubble on his chin, upper lip, and cheeks look as out of place as the long hair trailing over his collar. It hits me like a bomb. This is Jameson. I fly across the space separating us and pin him to the wall.

"Where did you come from?" I demand. "How did you send that message?"

Confusion on his face, he looks around the promenade. No one else has noticed him yet, and I'm thankful. The sooner Cassie and I move him to a less public place, the safer we are.

"Tell me where you were," I say. "There's no way you lived on Sub-Three for the last five years." I take and release a quick breath. The next question is harder, but I have to know. "Where's my dad?"

Jameson looks around the promenade again. "Am I on Canoples Station?" He focuses on the area around the tree. "Where's Pelham? I have to talk to Pelham. Have to do it before I forget."

The determination coming from him makes me just plain mad. For five long years, I believed my dad lost in a flitter accident. Then his second-in-command stumbles out of a lift and refuses to answer my questions.

Most teens on the Twelve Stations would have immediately called Security. I have something they don't, permission to handle the case from the head of Security. And I'll do just that. As soon as I finish interviewing the man who overrode my firewalls and activated a case file with a cryptic message, I will take him to the detention center where he belongs.

Hope reignites with Jameson's appearance. If he survived, my dad is somewhere close. I'm so sure of it I can feel the homecoming.

"Who are you?" He stares at me. "Do I know you? You have to find BD Bradford. I sent him a message. He'll want to talk to me."

Cassie gasps. In all the excitement, I forgot about her. I turn to her and shake my head. We need to know why he doesn't recognize me before we shock him with names.

"BD Bradford runs Canoples Investigations now," I say. "Why do you want to talk to him?"

"It's about his dad." He moans and presses a shaking hand against his head. "Forgetting. Can't forget." He glances at Cassie. "I know you. You're the pretty one. BD's girl. They want you." He drops his gaze to his boots. "Who am I?"

The first thing I notice is his boots are on the wrong side of worn. Jameson couldn't depend on those boots in vacuum for anything but trouble. Next, I catch a whiff of chemicals, like he has spent time in a space dust lab. Then … the biggest thing … he has no watch on his wrist, a necessity for anyone in Security. Their watches do more than tell time. Dispatch uses the device to notify officers of locations of trouble. They use them as communicators, and according to Wade, they can also speak a report into the watch after a situation is resolved.

The lights flicker, a very unusual event with all the backup systems on the generators. I check out the area around the tree in time to see Carl and Terry's stupefied expressions. Everyone looks up, but I glance to the side when something moves out of the corner of my eye.

An armored flitter races past the monster porthole giving everyone a view of Jupiter's malevolent red eye. This flitter looks nothing like the ones that gave everyone a great show a few hours ago. Laser blasts connect with the tetra-flex. Scorch marks appear. People scream.

A klaxon bursts into life. This klaxon is far different from the one I heard this morning. This klaxon means one of those lasers actually penetrated the porthole's tetra-flex!

Lessons learned from the weekly drills kick in. I reach into the back of the neck on my jumpsuit, yank out a hood, and then pull it over my head. Seconds later, I can breathe but not well. The oxygen regeneration system doesn't make sense to me even though everyone explains it whenever I complain. It has something to do with using filters I change weekly to take what I exhale and make it breathable again.

Flexing my wrists, I unlock the gloves in the sleeves of my suit and fasten them around my hands. My boots only require a tap of my big toe to bind against the sides of the faux leather. Properly protected, I turn to Cassie. She faces the portholes exposing the promenade to the spectacular view.

"The shields didn't come down." Her horrified voice echoes in my ear from the comm gear that's part of the suit.

"Head for the stairs before the bulkheads close," I yell.

I don't really need to do that, since we can hear each other by just talking. But my heart has taken off at high speed, and I'm about kick the first person I see responsible for our situation.

Jameson moans beside me. He sounds so strange I look at him. He hasn't activated his suit!

"Take him with you." I shove him toward her. "Put some moves in it, Cassie. We don't have much time."

"Stay safe." She drags him toward a stairwell. "I'll kick you clear to Pluto if you get hurt."

She really knows how to make a guy feel special.

I wait until she's safely inside the stairwell before turning my attention back to the emergency. The screams rise to a new level as others don their suits or stare in horror at the firefight going on right outside the portholes. Using my right thumb, I switch channels until the display in the upper left side of my hood indicates CI.

"Carl, Terry, are you there?"

"Sure am," Carl says.

"Have you five-by-five," Terry reports.

"Start moving people into the stairwells," I order. "I'll make sure no one's over here." I check out the area. "I don't see the Security pukes who gave me a hard time earlier. Where are they?"

"Left after losing three pay packets each," Carl says. "We're alone in here."

Security will be too busy in other parts of the station to send enough men up here to take care of the evacuation. It's up to my buds and me.

"Let's get moving," I say. "Carl, it's vitally important you get to where Cassie is. She just went into stairwell eight. Jameson's with her."

"On it." He starts shoving people in the right direction.

Terry begins directing people to the other stairwells. I point others to escape hatches, and hope we have enough time to get everyone off the promenade before the tetra-flex shatters.

CHAPTER SIXTEEN

A groaning cracking sound forces me to move faster. Very little time remains before everything comes apart. What's happening is so wrong an explanation will take a couple of light years, but here's the short version.

Every porthole on the station has protective covers capable of deflecting everything except a meteor. The massive tetra-flex porthole on the promenade has the latest state-of-the-art protection system on the Twelve Stations – lasers, a bulkhead as strong as the outer skin, and a shield for the interior.

Before my disbelieving eyes, another problem manifests. This one spells doom for everyone on the promenade. No matter what the threat, the bulkhead begins closing when sensors mounted around it detect a threat. Yet another emergency threatens the residents, and yet another safety equipment failure occurs. My already too long day stretches for at least another ten hours, and I have no idea what else to expect.

"No way," I mutter. "Don't think like that. Nothing else can go wrong. It just can't."

The echo of thuds rocks the area. I check out the direction they're coming from. Small bulkheads in front of the stairwell doors are sliding into place.

Finally! Something is going right, but we don't have much time to get people out of here.

Precious seconds I don't have pass as I key the com back to the overall channel.

"Everyone move to the other side of the promenade. Use the exits closest to the station's core," I shout over panicked questions. "The tetra-flex won't last much longer."

Another safety breakdown has occurred! No warning message blares from the speakers set into the ceiling. A few other people have noticed this failure. After pointing at the inset speakers, they move toward the exits. Stairwell doors open and close as the crowds push through them. Smaller kids fall, but thankfully someone always snatches them to safety. I take another quick look around the area. My heart stutters.

The tree's protective shield hasn't come down. A really stupid thing to worry about in the middle of a pirate attack, but that tree is a symbol of humans surviving after the evacuation from Earth. Yeah, it's replaceable, unlike me, but losing the tree today scares me. The certainty I have to save the aspen in addition to the last stragglers gives me a fearless feeling.

A mile and a half separates me from the control box. Most folks would say it's too much space to cross before I'm stuck inside the promenade after the tetra-flex shatters. For me, it is just a matter of pushing myself and proving I can take care of the situation without someone else's help.

"Hoppin' space rocks! Can't anything go right?"

I make my best time ever hoofing it over to the controls. Even then, I can't catch a break. After punching the controls three times and smacking my fist against the box a couple more, I finally hear the rumble of the shield moving upward. While keeping an eye on it, to make sure it seals, I search the tumbled chairs and tables, in case someone took cover under them. The arcades and food stands I don't worry about. They have rear exits the owners would have shooed everyone through as soon as they saw the tetra-flex crack.

My task complete, I turn in a circle. The tetra-flex of the huge porthole surrounds the entire station, giving a wonderful view of everything visible from this area. Today, numerous scorch marks and cracks mar the heavy cover, but they do nothing to block my view.

The scene outside takes on an aspect I never expected. Pirates chase passenger liners, but that only happens in deep space, usually near a dense nebula. I'm witnessing a tour shuttle, owned by Cassie and Carl's dad, trying to make the SpaceDock while no less than a dozen armored flitters chase it with lasers blazing. The blue and gold rising sun logo of Wills Expeditions blackens as strikes threaten to penetrate the skin. One flitter in particular catches my attention. I can't move, which is becoming more important with every passing second.

Bright red in the form of a mouth stretches over the pointed front end of the flitter with a jagged line of sharp teeth. A pair of crazed looking eyes covers the cockpit viewport. The tail appears as if someone decided to drive a serpent.

"Dad?" I scratch my head. "He's the only other one who knows the story. I think."

Even Wade doesn't know this, of that I am sure. Only days before Dad vanished, he took me for a stroll around the station. At the time, I was super proud of how he treated me like I was much older than ten. Our conversation comes back even though I need to push the memory aside and run for my life.

"No one else knows this," Dad had said. "My family didn't always uphold law and order. Back in the seventeenth century, we pirated treasure in the Caribbean. Old One Leg Bradford never achieved the fame of Blackbeard, but he sure did make enough to set up his family."

He had described the figurehead on our pirate ancestor's ship. It wasn't the usual woman. Old One Leg Bradford had used a fighting dragon – the same as the flitter attacking the shuttle!

Taking off at high speed, a clunk reminds me that I'm still in trouble, I race for the only stairwell door still open. A frightened cry beside the memorial tree stops me halfway there. I try to convince myself that I heard wrong but look back anyway and discover yet another problem, this one bigger than the rest.

"Where did he come from? I checked out the whole area."

A little boy cowers beside the fence. He is no more than six and doesn't have his protective suit on. I get back to the tree, and pull him into my arms. I pray with all my might that we make it before the bulkhead slams down and run. To my horror, the door starts lowering when I'm still five feet from it.

"Hang on," I yell at the kid and throw myself onto the deck, on my back.

Thank goodness for SpaceBall training. I slide into the stairwell and scramble to my feet before racing down to the next landing and pulling out the kid's gear. He remains frozen in place after I seal him into it.

"Need to keep going," I say in as calm a voice as I can manage. "Where's your shelter?"

"Sub-Two," he says.

"Do you know how to get there?" I ask.

"Yeah." He nods. "Thanks."

He runs off, and I switch to the Canoples Investigations private channel.

"Cassie, you there?" I call.

"Yeah. Carl and Terry almost knocked me over when they showed up. Where are you?" she asks.

"Uh." I look around, happy to see the large black two on the wall. "Stairwell two. You and the guys get over to Security. Take Jameson with you and corner Pelham. I'll explain when I get there."

"See you."

She clicks twice, indicating she has gone to another channel. Since we push the station rules by having one assigned to our agency, we can't talk privately. I start down the stairs, leaving the external receiver open so I can hear if someone else is in trouble.

Level eight, where Security is located, soon comes into view. I jab a keypad next to the door and release a relieved breath when it opens. So far, no one has changed the codes. That will happen as soon as Chief Pelham figures out that we have them. Then it will take me months to grab Wade's book again.

My buds wrestle a protesting Jameson through Security's door in front of me. I pick up the pace and join them. To my fury, Graham and Carson are at the desk. Jameson immediately breaks free and darts toward the doors.

"No you don't." I activate the bulkhead. "I don't want to look for you again."

He whimpers by the sealed door and watches Carson and Graham. I roll my eyes.

"Tell the chief we're here with what he wanted," I say.

"You don't order me around," Carson says. "The chief's busy right now with the pirate attack."

"I have ears only information," I say. "We need to get inside his office. Chief Pelham's orders."

"Sure." Graham laughs. "Tell me another fairy tale, Bradford. You're not a sworn Security Officer. You don't give orders around here."

I take a chance, since the last time I saw my bro he went to the hospital to interview Missy's parents.

"Wade, do you want everyone to know what you have on your wall in our quarters?" I yell at the top of my lungs.

He races toward me. His face is redder than Martian tomatoes; he's probably hotter than Uranus peppers, too.

"What?" he demands.

"I need to see the chief," I say. "It's about that thing he told you about this morning. Those losers from one of Saturn's work gangs." I point at Carson and Graham. "Are giving me grief."

"They'd probably do what you wanted if you didn't give them so much grief," Wade says. "Try please and thank you."

"You're not my mom or my dad," I say with a great deal of heat in my voice. "This is ears only. You heard the orders. I need to see Chief Pelham."

"This way." He points at the area behind the desk. "This had better be good. The tetra-flex just failed on the promenade. We're not sure everyone got out."

"Everyone's out." I grab Jameson's arm. "Canoples Investigations made sure of that before we left." I stare at him. "Hey, you're not wearing your suit. Why not?"

"Not needed in here." Wade smirks. "We're self-contained."

"Hah. Hah." I use my left thumb to release the facemask. It folds over my head and hangs down my back. "You could have told me before you did your pathetic Dad imitation."

I leave Jameson's mask on since Carson and Graham have fixed their beady eyes on him. Even more, the way they disappeared off the promenade right before the attack makes me wonder about their loyalty to Canoples Station's residents. Sure seems like I found yet another charity case. This one involves Security. Will this day ever end?

"Never," I mutter. "This day is doomed to last forever!"

CHAPTER SEVENTEEN

Carl, Terry, and Cassie shed their facemasks and walk toward the chief's office. I drag Jameson after them, and Wade brings up the rear.

"Make sure no one disturbs us," Wade snaps. "Don't release the bulkhead unless the chief tells you to. Tell the men patrolling the station that the promenade is clear."

"Why?" Carson asks. "Because your kid brother said it is. Didn't he just blow every bet against him by conspiring with his girlfriend?"

I spin around, ready to face months and months of psychs telling me I have to control my temper. No way will I let this pass.

"Big deal. You lost." Cassie's irritated voice floats back to us. "Learn your lesson. Don't ever bet against BD."

Her eloquent support warms me. The embarrassed expressions on Graham and Carson's faces almost make me keep my mouth shut. Except for one thing, the uncanny way they left the promenade right before the pirate attack.

"Or you actually feel guilty for leaving the promenade two minutes before the attack," I say.

"We didn't know that was about to happen," Carson says.

His eyes tell a very different story. In those uncaring gray eyes, I see guilt as clearly as if he had the word etched across them. I plan to discover how he and his loser partner knew about the attack as soon as possible.

"We had a lost child call," Graham claims. "A woman told us about the little boy right after Wills took our creds. She hadn't notified dispatch, yet."

"Yeah. Right." I shake my head in disbelief. "And I bet you'll dredge up a report to prove your point. Get real."

I drag Jameson into the short corridor leading to Pelham's office, and hope I did the right thing. With very few places on the station self-contained, not a whole lot of choices exist to hide him. The hospital is out; too many bumps, scrapes, and panic attacks will have the doctors and nurses hopping. Suggesting the space dock after what I saw will have everyone thinking I'm nuts.

We walk past a few confinement cells with their reinforced tetra-flex revealing no one inside them. Chief Pelham would have moved any prisoners to the holding area on Sub-Three as soon as the klaxon went off. I try to convince myself someone other than Dad knows about Old One Leg Bradford's figurehead, or the colors he used on his ship. The odds of that are less than slim. Our pirate ancestor never made the history vids, and only family interested in our Earth relations knows about him – Dad and me.

"What are you thinking?" Wade asks. "Don't tell me nothing. You look like you ate a rotten Gut-Buster."

No one ever says he's blind or dumb. *Well, probably dumb, but definitely not blind.* He's probably my best bet for a fast denial of the thoughts bombarding my mind.

"Did Dad talk to you about Old One Leg Bradford?" I ask.

"Who's that? Another one of your Gut-Buster nightmares? You need to give up those pizzas. They're no good for you."

Well, I have my answer. Not the one I want, and it leaves me with a strong suspicion. That has to wait until Pelham hears my report before saying anything where anyone other than my group can hear.

"Didn't think so." I march into the chief's office. "Jameson showed up on the promenade right before the pirate attack." I deactivate the man's hood. "There's something else. Dad's alive. I think he was piloting one of the flitters attacking Mr. Wills' tour ship. Did it land okay?"

"No more damage other than a few scorch marks, and one very angry pilot. The passengers thought the attack was part of the tour." A smile flits across Chief Pelham's lips. "You've done more in a few hours than I have in five years. Tell me why you think Tom's alive."

"What do you mean someone attacked one of Dad's ships?" Cassie stares at Jameson. "You said he wanted me. I was supposed to fly today. Are you telling us that someone wanted to kidnap me?"

Most guys would leap to their girl's defense. Not me. I kick back and let her rant. Jameson had better start spilling what he knows fast. Cassie is fearsome when she is angry.

"Who are you?" He looks around in confusion. "Where am I? I have to get to Canoples Station and find BD Bradford. It's very important. He holds the key to stopping Old One Leg."

Wade's mouth drops open, and he faces me. I point a finger at my chest.

"Me? I don't have a clue," I say.

Right. I know. Well, I suspect. But I can't do anything about it until I figure out a few things. That will happen as soon as we can get into our office to brainstorm.

That isn't happening any time soon. Before Chief Pelham authorizes raising the bulkheads, he has to make sure no one else will attack the station. While the governor usually gives orders, right now Security is in charge. *Thank goodness.* Governor Tulane, Lisa's dad, does nothing without a dozen committees telling him if it's cost effective, won't damage the station's environment, and no one will suffer emotional issues that might cause them to turn into mentals. We have no time for a discussion group to debate for months.

"Okay." Chief Pelham runs his hands through his hair. "We'll find a place to stow Jameson. Obviously, he's been on the station, but we don't know where. BD, did you get a chance to check out Sub-Three?"

"Nope." I grin. "I decided to grovel first. It worked."

"Yeah. Right," Cassie shoots at me. "If that's groveling, I'd hate to see humility." She smiles. "But I liked it, and I already gave back the creds. They're in your account. I just wanted to see if you still wanted me around."

Girls, what can I say about them? Confusing doesn't even begin to describe them.

"What creds?" Wade asks.

"Do you think I work for free?" I ask. "Governor Jackson paid us for finding Chuckles." I face Chief Pelham. "And don't tell me it was an illegal transaction. He paid us for a job his wife hired us to do. As soon as we realized he had something illegal, we contacted you."

"You did." The chief nods. "I won't confiscate the creds, but I warn you. Governor Jackson and his wife threatened to file a claim for a refund through the business council. They say you tricked them."

"They had an illegal re-kat," I protest. "Is he trying to stiff us? No way."

"You have a point." Pelham's smile widens. "As I told him. So, I want you and the rest of Canoples Investigations to stay close to my office until the current situation is under control."

"Wait." I hold up a hand. "There's one more thing. Old One Leg."

Jameson's head bobs up and down. He looks at me with scared eyes.

"Old One Leg wants the girl," he whispers, the side of his left eye twitching. "She'll make BD Bradford come out of hiding. The old man wants BD to do something."

"I'm BD Bradford," I say. "Yeah, I know. I'm not the scrawny, short kid you knew five years ago. So, tell me. Just who is Old One Leg?"

He looks me up and down. Since I have grown more than a foot in the last five years and developed a lot of muscle, he takes a long time examining me.

"You sure don't look like BD," he finally says. "Prove you're him."

"Dad told me about Old One Leg Bradford a few days before he left." I slip a hand into a pocket and touch a medallion I keep pinned to the inside of the fabric. "He gave me the only thing Old One Leg had when he died in New Orleans with Jean Lafitte at his side."

Jameson nods. He finally believes me, but his eyes bother me. They look like he'll deliver his message and nothing else. We need information, more than a message. I have to come up with a way to pry the secrets out of him.

"Doesn't really have only one leg." Jameson rocks from side to side and stares at the ceiling. "Has both legs. Flies like a charnel bird from Earth. Quick, harsh, and make the kill – that's his motto."

"Who is he talking about?" Wade asks.

"Shhh!" I hold up a hand. "Did Old One Leg say where he got the idea for his flitter's paint job?"

Chief Pelham leans forward on his elbows. "What paint job?"

"I'll explain in a minute," I say. "Jameson, you have to tell me what Old One Leg wants."

Instead of answering, his eyes roll back in his head. He goes stiff as a board and falls backward, slamming into the deck. Wade beats me to his side and checks his pulse.

"He's alive," he says. "I'll attach him to the med-strips and have a doctor in emergency do a quick check."

There is more than one way to have someone checked on the Twelve Stations, but this method requires the person be in custody. I guess I can say Jameson is. He sure isn't going anywhere.

Wade hooks up the leads and opens a channel to the hospital's emergency room. A few minutes later, a voice comes over the speakers.

"Whoever that patient is," a doctor says, "we need him in here fast. I have electrical readings indicating he's suffering from the effects of a hallucinogenic drug."

Space Dust! It's the first thing to pop into my head. Pirates dealt with treasure in the seventeenth and eighteenth century. After Dad told me about my ancestor, I spent a lot of time studying them. The only treasure now is what idiots use to make themselves happy, or so they call it. Space dust is as addictive as meth was in the twenty-first century.

"Prep him, Wade," Chief Pelham says. "Pick a team to guard Jameson at all times. Wait until they get here to transport him."

While Wade prepares Jameson for transport, I walk over to a porthole. A bulkhead covers the view, but I need time without anyone interrupting me to put together what I heard.

Dad flew like a charnel bird. He loved everything about Old One Leg Bradford, but he left out some very important information about our infamous ancestor. I wonder if he cared about that part.

On my own, I discovered why Old One Leg died broke. Sure, he looted merchant ships, but he donated the booty to poor communities all over the Gulf of Mexico. He was a hero, unlike Dad. I now suspect he lives a fantasy life based on his imagination.

"BD, you'll have to clear something up for me," Chief Pelham says.

"What?" I face him.

"When you got here and yelled, Wade looked like he wanted to strangle you. Just what does he have on his wall that would upset him so badly?" He leans back in his chair and steeples his fingers under his chin. "What's so bad it would make him turn the color of Venusmuts?"

"Don't you dare!" Wade points at me. "Say a word, and Mom'll find out about how you ignored Missy."

Before the attack, that might have kept the secret buried forever. Right about now, I'm not feeling too kindly toward him. I have about had it with his threats and constant imitation of a dad who has, I suspect, thrown away his life to have fun.

"So?" I shrug. "We more than made up for it when we evacuated the promenade."

"He has a point." Chief Pelham smiles. "Spill."

"It's a live-vid-pic of Jenna Rock in concert," I say. "Signed. He met her after the concert here last year, and they went on a date."

"That's worth more than ten thousand creds," Terry says, envy dripping from his voice.

"I want one," Carl says. "Can I see yours, Wade?'

"No." Wade glares at me. "No one sees it. I promised Jenna after she gave it to me."

He puts a lot of challenge into his glare. A challenge no younger brother can ignore. Not many people know Jenna Rock sneaks aboard Canoples as Mildred Casey every couple of weeks. She and Wade see each other constantly but never admit their relationship to anyone. Their careers make the publicity too much to handle. As he narrows his eyes and mouths a threat to tell Mom about the whole Missy incident, my temper boils.

I just can't let him get away with that. "He kisses the live-vid-pic every night."

Not every night that I know of, but it doesn't matter now. From the laughter, my always-perfect older brother will never hear the end of this.

CHAPTER EIGHTEEN

Snickers outside the door anger me, and I understand Chief Pelham's concern about making sure no one hears us talking about this unusual case. The secret I exposed is now in the brains of two men who love to embarrass Wade, and they will do just that the rest of his life, along with spreading vicious rumors about his relationship with Jenna Rock.

"Sorry." I walk to the door. "I'll make sure Carson and Graham don't tell anyone."

"How?" Wade asks. "You can't take back what you said."

"Too true." I open the door. "But I can make them understand they'll never feel safe as long as I'm around."

Carson and Graham make kissing noises in the air. Neither has grown beyond the mental age of a jock in the locker room.

I glance at Wade. A red flush rises from his neck to the top of his head.

Oh! This won't happen.

I harass my big brother. That keeps us sane. No one else will have the opportunity to humiliate him.

"Hey!" I yell. "Do you want everyone to know you hid in Security during the attack? Must be a lot of folks from the promenade wondering why four teens did your job while you shuffled micro-chips."

Graham chokes off his kissing sound. Carson gulps. They look at someone behind me.

"Well done, BD," Chief Pelham says. "Very good."

His super quiet voice sends a serious scare through every inch of my body. He's very low key until something upsets him. Even then, it's hard to tell he's angry because he never yells.

"If you're finished listening at closed doors," he says. "I strongly suggest you return to your duties. Check with the officers at their posts. Find out if the threat has ended, and if there were any injuries during the evacuation to the shelters."

Graham takes off so fast he trips over his boots. Carson holds out a memory stick.

"Final reports from the skin zone incident, sir," Carson says. "We had to wait for the hospital to forward theirs."

Chief Pelham takes the stick and shuts the door.

"Wade, run another medical check on Jameson." He sits at his desk. "BD, I think you'd better hold onto any other information you discover about your brother. Certain revelations can make his job difficult."

"Okay." Heat flames across my face. "Won't happen again."

I pace around the room and review my clues. Nothing about today feels normal; nothing repeats as all these weird things keep happening, except one thing. The pirates attacked the station twice. That and what happened to Missy and her parents bring new rumors to mind.

Some of the teens will try anything new. A few indicated a great party ship will show up in a couple of weeks, to await Io's eruption.

Stopping next to my buds, I wrack my brain to recall what I overheard on the promenade last week.

"Have any of you received an invite to that ship. The … the." I snap my fingers. "Uh … the Star Traveler?"

"Shredded it," Cassie says. "Lisa wanted me to go, but I don't do that junk."

That junk can only mean one thing – Space Dust. Nothing else elicits such a strong response from her.

"That's what I figured." I smile. No one will make my girl take drugs. "Thanks. You just helped me put something together."

We keep our voices low. Me, because I'm not ready to reveal what I suspect. I figure she's following my lead.

While worrying about a space dust problem taking over the lives of some of my classmates, I find something else to bother me. My stomach rumbles and growls. Since it's way past the time I snack in the morning and have lunch, I know how to solve that problem. One little problem though, my fav pizza joint just closed down indefinitely.

A Gut-Buster will give me the chance to think, while also clearing the room of Graham and Carson if they decide to stick their noses into my business. The more I think about the round, eighteen-inch doughy disk covered with tomato sauce and topped with every single vegetable, meat, and cheese that exists the more my mouth waters. I imagine cupping both hands lovingly under the crust and lifting several slices … no, a whole pizza to my mouth. The scent I know so well tantalizes my brain until I can no longer stand it.

"Do you have a frozen Gut-Buster?" I demand.

Not as good as fresh pizza from a real oven, but the micro-cooked variety will calm my frayed nerves.

"Hungry?" Chief Pelham asks.

"I'm two meals behind, and it doesn't look like I'll have time for dinner," I respond. "At seventeen, that's the end of the galaxy."

He laughs and leans out the door. "Carson, cook up a couple dozen Gut-Busters and bring them in here. We have a bunch of teens with holes in their stomachs."

Even when Dad ran Security, I never understood how a chief can treat a suspect like everything is on the up and up. Just doesn't sit right to make nice to a criminal to get information from them. But will I argue about someone providing me enough Gut-Busters to fill me up for a couple of hours?

Do I look stupid? More than a few people, like Graham and Carson, think I am. They don't know me very well.

While we wait, Terry and Wade read Jameson's message. I stand at a porthole, a normal sized one, and go over the sight of that flitter.

Hoppin' space rocks, it looks just like what Dad described only days before he disappeared.

There is even a drawing of it in one of the family books Mom keeps in our quarters.

Jameson's statement, the only sensible one he made, echoes in my head. Is he referring to Old One Leg Bradford? The pirate died centuries ago. Ghosts don't come back to life. Most especially, ghosts don't find where their ancestors moved to after Earth's evacuation.

How can the pirate find us? Will he know how to control a flitter? The small spacecraft are state-of-the-art as far as a two person craft goes. Finger controls allow a pilot to fly from any part of the ship. Some have laser blasters mounted on them, but the person ordering one has to have a Security code to buy it. The laws are real tough about anyone owning a weapon if they aren't part of law enforcement.

As I trace a finger in an elliptical pattern on the porthole, I wonder how a bunch of pirates put their hands on one of those armored flitters let alone a fleet and more importantly, the hotshot lasers on them. Wade might give me a hard time, but he sure would have said something about those going missing.

"It isn't right," I whisper.

"You say something?" Carl joins me.

"Where's Cassie?"

"Helping Terry and Wade," he says. "What's eating you?"

"The flitter." I stare at Jupiter's mass. No one lives there, but according to rumors pirates built a nest on the surface. "Did you see it?"

"Too busy getting people into the stairwells," Carl says. "What's so important about a flitter?"

"The nose," I say in a near whisper. "It's just like Old One Leg Bradford's figurehead on his ship."

"What?" Carl pulls me around to face him. "Who is Old One Leg Bradford? Jameson only said Old One Leg,"

"Something Dad said right before he disappeared," I say.

I try to remember everything about that day. As it happened seven years ago, I have a hard time dredging up the memories. Mostly, I had been happy to have him taking me on his rounds. At the time, I had this idea of taking his job after going to security academy on Mars for a degree in law enforcement. The questions I asked Dad had to do with a ten-year-old's perception of working in Security.

A smile tilts my lips as one comes to mind. I wanted to know how long someone had to stay on Fomalhaut for holding up the pizza place. Dad said a crime that despicable deserved a life sentence. Sure makes sense to me, both then and now.

The most wonderful smell in the galaxy wafts into the room. Carl and I ram into each other in our haste to make it to Chief Pelham's desk first. To my amazement, there are three dozen Gut-Busters on the tray, several stacked on top of each other.

"That's hot!" Terry yells.

He has just shoved half of one into his mouth. I pick up two and take a bite.

Boy, he is right.

Fanning my mouth, I chew as fast as I can.

"Gross!" Cassie sets a piece on a plate and takes a fork from the chief.

Talk about disgusting. Who eats the best pizza on Canoples Station with a fork? Folks all over the galaxy come here on their vacations to sample the Gut-Buster. I ignore the glare she always gives me when she hates how I'm acting and finish my first double-stacked pizza. Picking up another two, I take a deep breath and release it before diving in. Before I have gone through half, the sound of shouting voices interrupts my lunch.

That's a felony of the worst degree.

CHAPTER NINETEEN

Carl, Terry, and I snatch several Gut-Busters each and stuff the pieces into our mouths. None of us does more than chomp once or twice before swallowing.

"Slow down," Cassie says. "You'll get sick or get–" Her voice drops to a low, troubled whisper. "Gas."

She has a very good reason to warn us. The guys and I loaded up on Gut-Busters before an important test a couple of months ago, on purpose of course. The consequences were horrendous, and made us miss a case almost as important as our current one. We swore off another gorge session after we found ourselves confined to a room on Sub-One until we no longer polluted the station's air or gagged each other. We asked her to warn us if we were about to end up in the same predicament. However, she has no clue what we've done since she quit hanging around. To keep from gagging each other again, we devised a cure.

"I have them." Carl dumps three packets in the middle of Chief Pelham's desk. "Hurry."

The three of us grab one packet each. While Carl and Terry swallow the contents in one gulp and wince when the taste hits their tongues, I sprinkle the powder across six more Gut-Busters and dive into the rest of my meal. No use wasting good eating time taking the cure, a mixture of parsley, cinnamon, and lavender. Nothing ruins the taste of a pizza piled up with more toppings of every variety than it has crust.

"Just looking at you three makes me sick." Chief Pelham puts his slice down. "You're going through that food faster than an asteroid through a flitter's skin."

"Thanks," I mumble around a mouthful. "Nice to know you think we can do something right."

"That wasn't a compliment," he says and shakes his head when I grab the last three pizzas. "Ugh."

The loud voices outside the room get louder. Raised voices can only mean trouble to the max. Nothing will interrupt the only food I might get my hands and teeth on today.

"Tell Chief Pelham that Governor Tulane is out here," a man hollers. "Governor Jackson and I need to discuss those hooligans from Canoples Investigations with him."

I finish my food and look for something to clean up with. During my speedy lunch, I must have dropped the toppings from at least one of the pizzas onto my jumpsuit. The sight of so many vegetables and meats decorating my chest becomes too much to bear. After carefully knocking them into my hand, I toss the spillage into my mouth and chew quickly but not fast enough. The two governors come through the door before I swallow.

"Chief, do you really expect me to overlook this?" Governor Tulane demands.

He and Governor Jackson stop right inside the door. I glance at Terry and Carl. They're in the process of cleaning the mess off their jumpsuits, about three minutes behind me. I grin.

"Slow gets you in trouble every time." I glance at the governors. "Just to set the record straight before you put down me and my friends. Mrs. Jackson i-mailed Canoples Investigations in a panic because she lost a travel bag. She told us there were toiletries in it. Whatever they are."

"What a woman needs to make herself beautiful," Governor Tulane says.

Who is he kidding? From what I saw of her, she needs to ask for a refund.

"She needs to use more," I say in my most helpful voice but laughter makes me snort on the last word. "Or get a refund. That stuff didn't work."

"You don't understand," he says. "Women work hard to please us men."

Ah, I've done it.

It doesn't take much to distract him. Since his daughter is as dumb as he is, I have a lot of practice.

"All right, BD, don't make matters worse." Chief Pelham shakes his head again. "Governor Jackson, Canoples Investigations followed the rules I set for their charter when they contacted me about the illegal re-kat your wife had in the travel bag. They didn't break the law, you and your wife did." The chief clears his throat. "You used teens to find something she lost without informing them about the contraband. They risked their lives to bring it back to her, and then you paid them a bribe to keep their mouths shut."

My mouth falls open. How does he know about the extra creds the governor gave us? I never told him. Another glance at Terry and Carl does nothing to clear up the mystery. They look as confused as I feel.

A puzzle to solve at another time, but I can guess the answer. Chief Pelham always figures out what we're up to, and he hinted at having been as bad as we are. He probably pulled the very same stuff we do now when he was a kid.

Involuntary shudders work up and down my spine at that image. A face like the chief's on a kid will scare off the worst space pirate. He's pretty cool and helps us whenever he can, but his face looks like he wrestles rocks in the rings orbiting Saturn.

"I paid them nine hundred creds to keep quiet," Governor Jackson protests. "They took my money and turned in my wife's re-kat anyway. That's not right. I want a refund."

Nobody says he's the brightest light in the galaxy. He confesses to a crime while trying to bilk us out of our fee.

Talk about stupid.

Next time I agree to a recovery case, I'll make sure the client doesn't need written instructions on how to use the refresher.

"Well, BD?" Chief Pelham asks. "Is there any truth to this?"

"Terry and Carl weren't there when I made the agreement with Governor Jackson *truth!*," I say. "The governor gave me the money and made the deal *truth!*. You and Wade showed up before I could tell them about it." *Three truths in a row! A first, and the biggest miracle ever to happen!*

"Got that straight," Terry says. "Carl and I walked off to report possibly seeing a locator beacon in the skin area. We also informed Chief Pelham about the contraband. BD never got the chance to tell us about the deal."

Governor Tulane clears his throat and smooths back his thin blonde hair. My buds and I have bets down on his going bald by the end of the year unless he stops playing with his hair. It's his signature move whenever he's about to make what he calls an executive decision. I put a hand protectively over the pocket containing my creds. No way will I give them up. Since Cassie returned what she blackmailed out of me, I have enough for the game.

"Well, Governor Jackson?" Chief Pelham asks. "Is this true?"

"But I paid them to stay quiet," Governor Jackson says. "They should have lied instead of letting you terrorize my wife with threats of a hefty fine and a week in jail. Then you had the audacity to take Chuckles. He's a very sensitive re-kat. He'll pine away in impound."

From what I saw, Chuckles can do without whatever the Jackson's feed him. That re-kat is the fattest one I have ever come across. His presence explains the heavy travel bag that almost made me take a thirty-five hundred foot fall.

"Chas, why don't we visit Chuckles," Governor Tulane suggests. "It's only for a few days. He'll be with you and Rita soon."

Talk about a change of heart! We skate past the trouble without having to do anything but tell the truth. I breathe a sigh of relief.

Wait just a minute!

Governor Jackson admitted to breaking quarantine regulations. Why does he get away with announcing their intentions to ignore the rules the Ruling Council makes? The same laws the rest of us have to obey or pay a huge fine and face punishment for even thinking about ignoring them.

"You can't visit Chuckles," I say.

"Young man, you don't have the authority to tell me what we can and cannot do," Governor Tulane says. "Our position gives us certain privileges."

Now I know why Lisa acts like she does.

"Governor Jackson, I did you a favor," Chief Pelham says. "Ignore one more rule, visit your re-kat, and I'll charge you, your wife, and your personal protection detail with using physical violence on two Security officers to avoid quarantine regulations."

"You have no proof," Governor Jackson says.

"We do." Carl holds up his PocketPad. "I think this belongs on the 'net." He grins evilly. "The Twelve Stations 'net not the local one."

The screen replays the fight in vivid detail. Both governors back away and apologize for having bothered us. While leaving, their eyes linger on the corner where Jameson lies on a stretcher.

With that situation finally finished, I turn my attention to the one blasting through our lives as surely as if the lasers that destroyed the tetra-flex on the promenade sliced through us.

"Chief, except for the promenade, the station's safe now," Graham says from the doorway. "Governor Jackson asked if you'd return power to him."

My heart leaps into my mouth. One thing still isn't resolved. I turn to Chief Pelham and open my mouth.

"No," the chief says. "I can't return the station to the governor for a few more hours, but I will release the residents from the shelters. Be sure to inform everyone to avoid the promenade until repairs are complete."

Phew! Safe. Or are we?

The mystery behind the pirate attack, and who leads them, still bugs me. My buds and I have to dive into work to find out what is going on. There isn't much time to do it, either.

How do I know? The old BD-Bradford-gut-feeling is how. It always lets me know when things are about to turn upside down, and it's going in high gear. Or the cure might have failed. I did eat my weight and more in Gut-Busters.

CHAPTER TWENTY

I jerk my head at my buds and then the door. They nod. Now that they understand my immediate need, I face the chief.

"We'll be in our office," I say. "Cassie and Terry will work on the message. Carl and me … well let's just say we have something else to check out."

"What?" Wade asks.

Always suspicious, always on my case for some reason or another, but that's my big brother. His self-appointed role as my walking, talking conscience bugs the life out of me, and I see no way to stop him. This time, I can't clue him in on what I have running through my head. Before I trust anyone except my buds with the information, I have to make sure I'm right.

"I'll tell you later." I move toward the door, my buds on my heels. "Don't try to pry it out of me, Wade. Your girlfriends might hear about their competition."

To keep his relationship with Jenna Wade on the QT, he dates almost every night he isn't on duty. There are a large number of women his age who compete to be seen with him.

No real need exists to threaten him since news spread faster on

Canoples Station than space flu, but I want him to wonder if I'll embarrass him. The best way in the universe to keep him off my back pops into my head. One day, he'll learn to use tougher passwords on his PerSys, but for now I'm thankful he refuses to listen to my advice.

"I wonder how fast the scandal-vids can get here," I say. "I'm sure they'd love to know all about Jenna's visit last weekend.

"If I hear a word," he says.

His voice holds all kinds of threats, starting with twisting my body into the shape of a Venus-mut, and ending with him telling Mom everything he believes I have ever done wrong. His unspoken promise to create problems no longer scares me.

"Yeah. Yeah." I wave a hand over a shoulder. "You'll be too busy avoiding the vultures (what we call the reporters and videographers who go after celebs). Don't threaten me, big bro. Or everyone finds out how often your girl shows up and what name she uses."

Wade's roar of anger cuts off when the chief's door slides closed.

"You really need to lay off Wade," Terry says.

"When the sun goes nova," I say. "He's enough of a jerk already. He'd get worse if I didn't give him a hard time."

As we walk into the reception area, two things immediately catch my attention. Governors Jackson and Tulane are talking to Jameson in a corner. Then I stare at Carson and Graham. The dynamic duo grins as Jameson keeps trying to make sense. But I have no memory of him leaving the chief's office.

"Chief," I holler. "How did Jameson get out here?"

What's going on around here? Has someone slipped in one of those sci/fi vid special effects? Is there a secret entrance to the chief's office? Did I miss something while I stood at the porthole? Even though I wasn't looking, I would have heard Jameson moving. He isn't exactly quiet.

The governors race for the door. Carl and Terry block their path, and a loud argument erupts.

"Move or you'll find yourself on Fomalhaut," Governor Tulane threatens. "Don't think I won't do it."

Chief Pelham and Wade run into the room.

"This has become far too repetitive," Chief Pelham says. "No one boards Fomalhaut without a hearing I initiate. Governor, and I don't care which one of you answers, why did you use the bolt hole?"

Ah, that explains Jameson's mysterious movement. Not! A bolthole?

It makes sense, but I have never heard of one on the station, and I pride myself on knowing every shortcut and hiding place. Never know when they'll come in handy.

"It's my right to know about threats to the station." Governor Tulane pats his sleeve hems with his fingertips. All he succeeds in doing is activating his survival gloves. "Oh my!"

"If there was a viable threat, I would have informed you." Chief Pelham frowns. "Wade, escort Jameson to the hospital. Tell his detail absolutely no visitors unless I approve them."

Wade takes Jameson toward the prisoner lift in a corner while the chief points at the exit. Graham and Carson beat feet out the door.

"They're trouble," I say. "Don't know why but they're trouble."

"Don't get involved," Chief Pelham says. "Why don't you kids take off? I'll handle the governors' determination to make the current threat worse." He grins. "Speaking to them about helping instead of hindering will certainly make my day so much better."

The expressions of sheer terror on the troublemaking governors faces leaves me with an image I file for a time when I need a good laugh. While I don't want to leave, so I can witness what I'm sure will be the best chewing out I've ever heard, I have a way to discover what will happen. To do that, I have to activate a bug I hid in Security months ago, which will land me in hotter steam than I have ever been in – if anyone finds it.

"Come on," I say to my buds. "We're out of here."

It only takes seconds to deactivate the bulkhead blocking us from entering our office. As soon as we're inside, I look around in stunned amazement. Someone has broken in!

"Where's the PerSys?" Cassie asks. "Did you move it?"

"No way." I stare in stupefied horror at the blank spot on my desk.

We have the smallest office on Canoples Station. It was nothing more than a supply closet when Chief Pelham approved it for our use. After we cleaned out about two centuries worth of junk, we made it space-efficient by building countertop desks. All of us sit in a line facing the door. Discussions are fun. I usually have a sore neck after one.

"What happened?" Carl asks. "It's only been five hours since we went up to the luxury level to find that bag. I feel like I've lived a week."

My feelings exactly. This morning started with a minor pirate attack and has done nothing but get worse since.

"At least I transferred the message to my PocketPad," I mutter. "We still have that."

Cassie's mouth falls open. "You transferred it instead of forwarding it?"

"Sure." I look at her. "Is that important?"

Computers run our lives. So much so, I never think about the tech stuff unless Cassie and Terry aren't around. That happens rarely. Carl and I handle the legwork while they do the background and searches. It's what makes us so great. We all know what we do best, and never argue about who has to handle the nasty stuff.

"Important?" Cassie yanks my PocketPad out of its holster and opens the mail function. "Of course it's important. That means you kept all the original sending information! We have a great lead on where Jameson was when he sent this."

She and Terry huddle in a corner and mumble. It sounds like tech-geek, a language now taught in school, so I ignore them. Carl blows out a frustrated breath.

"It's great they can trace the message, but we still need our PerSys," he says. "It has all our cases on it."

"I backed up last night," I say. "Except for the re-kat thing and

Jameson's case, we have everything saved on a stick."

It's not really a stick, but that's what we call our memory chips. They hold up to fifty-thousand tera-gigs of data on a plastic coated stick the length of my little finger.

"Good." He stares at the mess on our communal desk. "Will you call the chief, or do you want me to?"

"I'll do it." I dart out the door. "Bet Wade gives me a hard time so I'll save your ears. See you when he quits flapping his jaws."

My feet drag as I return to Security. All the while, I wonder who took our PerSys. The emergency means the SpaceDock is in lockdown. No one can come on or leave Canoples until Chief Pelham approves it so our PerSys is still close.

I push my way inside, ignore the jerks at the desk, and go toward the chief's office.

"You can't go back there," Carson yells. "That's for official personnel only."

"Go find a Venus-mut," I mutter. "Why can't you stay away from me?"

After shoving the chief's door open, I lean against it. Wade and Chief Pelham look up.

"You set a speed record," I say.

"That's what happens when you plan ahead." Wade hooks an arm over his chair back. "You look like you're about to spit rivets. What's up?"

"Someone stole our PerSys," I say. "Don't ask how they got it. The bulkhead was still sealed when we got there."

"Great." He shakes his head. "Now we'll never know where Jameson was when he sent that message."

"Yeah, you will," I say. "So don't call me a computer dummy anymore." Like I care, but always-by-the-book Wade will never say something unless it's true. "Cassie and Terry are checking out my PocketPad right now. I transferred the message instead of forwarding it. That means we can trace it."

Hey! I just sounded like I know what I'm talking about.

This is another first in a day full of them.

"Wonders will never cease," Chief Pelham says. "I suppose you kids touched everything on the door going in, didn't you?"

"We didn't know," I say.

"Of course you didn't," he says. "Okay, I'll walk back with you. Wade, take over here. Yell if something comes up."

"BD, I had to tell Mom about the promenade. Better get ready," Wade says.

What a threat!

Now that Mom knows I was the last person off the promenade, she'll hit the ceiling and keep going until she's far from the station. I might have a reprieve while she finds her way back, but it won't take long. Her favorite activity is giving me a hard time about all the chances I take.

Like other teens, I never think about risking life and limb to have fun. When will she give me a break?

153

CHAPTER TWENTY-ONE

Chief Pelham and I make it back into Canoples Investigations just as Terry whoops. He does a couple of loopy things with wires he attaches to my PocketPad and yells even louder.

"I found it! Jameson sent this from 6-G-245." Terry exclaims.

That translates to level six, corridor G, quarters two-forty-five – where I live. My heart jumps into my mouth and stays there. I can't talk even if I want to. Chief Pelham drops a hand onto my shoulder.

"I'm sure there's a good reason," the chief says. "I know you didn't send the message, BD."

So am I. Sure I had nothing to do with sending the message. How can I explain?

"That's BD's place," Cassie says. "Keep looking. I'm betting this jerk bounced the signal. He probably used open systems to hide where he actually was."

Calm replaces my panic. She's right. Mom is forever telling me to turn off our HomeSys, in addition to my Port-A-Sys. I connected my portable system to the one in the office to finish a report last night.

"That's how the message got here," I say. "A hijack."

Hijackers search the station's intranet for open systems. They use the victim's computer to conduct illegal business or send viruses to dummies that open the i-mails for a quick cred.

"You didn't," Carl says. "BD, you could have finished this morning. Your mom meant it when she told us we had to slow down. She'll flip when she finds out."

"Already did. About ten minutes after I started. No big." I shrug. "She'll get over it."

"Angela rarely gets over anything related to you," Chief Pelham says. "Don't push her, BD. She's having a hard time at work lately. With Tom's possible reappearance, she'll snap at the smallest problem. Remember that before you blow off what she tells you to do."

When Dad disappeared, and everyone thought he died, Chief Pelham comforted Mom. I gave both of them a hard time until I figured out something my parents never mentioned. She and Dad were about to file for divorce. I never knew why but understood Chief Pelham made her happy and accepted him as someone I trusted long ago.

That's a lie. It was only last year when I stopped harassing them. Now I can't wait for their wedding next month.

"Chief, about the flitter I mentioned," I say.

"Not now," he says.

"Now." I lean against the long desk. "See, Dad told me something. I already explained that, but with Jameson calling the pirate leader Old One Leg, it's too much of a coincidence. My pirate ancestor was Old One Leg Bradford. Dad admired him."

"BD, Tom died five years ago," Chief Pelham says. "We may not have found a body, but we don't always."

"Or Dad planned it." I press a fist against my eyes. "When did the pirates first show up around Canoples?"

"Six years ago," he says quietly. "About the time Tom and Angela started talking about a divorce." He pulls my hand down. "Do you know what you're saying?"

"Yeah."

And I know, with everything inside me, I have to accept it fast.

"Well, since you understand, I guess you know what I'm about to tell the four of you," Chief Pelham says. "Especially you, Cassie."

Oh, do I know what Chief Pelham is about to say, and I will fight him as hard as I can.

"Ah no!" I protest. "We're not little kids. It's not like we need help putting on our gear. You don't have to protect us."

"Yes, I do." He jerks his head at the door. "Close down the office until I figure this out. Go home. Stay there."

"I have to fly for Dad later," Cassie says. "He'll hit his rest period before our last tour. We don't have another qualified pilot."

"I just opened the SpaceDock," Chief Pelham says. "Your passengers might take one of the transports to Mistlich, to avoid more problems with the pirates."

"They didn't. Dad already messaged me," she says. "I told him okay. If you ground me, he'll lose the creds, and a very important contract."

"I'll have someone go with you," Chief Pelham says. "The rest of you, I know you'll burn up air time talking on your computers, so you can stay at BD's. I'll stay with you until we know for sure if his hunch is right."

Oh, so it's just a hunch, is it? Well, I'll find a way to prove it's true.

We close up the office. I activate the notice board on the door, so any prospective customers know where to contact us. So what if it's not what Chief Pelham wants? If someone shows up paying creds for us to locate something, we'll jet as soon as they agree to the contract.

"Ready?" He smiles at us. "I talked with Wade while you took your time. Someone's meeting us up top to go with Cassie."

"You don't have to do that," she says. "I can take care of myself."

"I'm sure you can," he says. "Just give this old man a few less gray hairs today and go along with me. BD might be right. Until I figure out what Jameson meant about someone wanting you, I'll have an officer with you."

It feels like we skipped out of school to hang at the arcades with the chief making sure we keep our mouths closed on the walk to the lift. Once inside, he uses an override to keep the lift moving until it reaches level six, where all of us live in Hallway G. Jan Wilson, a friend of Wade's, steps inside and continues up to the SpaceDock with Cassie. The rest of us walk away. I have a sensation of something wrong.

Sure, she has gone her own way for a while, but she can handle anything. If I admit the truth, she can out fly all of us, and that's on a bad day. No matter how hard I try to push the words out of my brain, they remain stuck. Someone wants her, and I have a pretty good idea who that someone is.

A couple of guys from school smirk at us when they see our escort. Fat chance they might have missed seeing Chief Pelham. A person has to be blind to miss Security's pukey green uniforms.

"Hey, BD," Tony Adams says. "I hear you messed up good this time."

"In your dreams," I mutter.

I'll never live this down. He gossips worse than Lisa. Come to think of it, he hangs with her. Must be where he learned it.

Once we are inside my quarters, I raid the kitchen for food. Since the governors cut my lunch short, I still need something to finish filling the hole in my stomach. Mom went on a healthy eating kick a couple of months ago. All I can locate are fruit or veggie treats in the cooler. The cupboards aren't much better. No cookies or anything else loaded with chemicals and no nutritional value.

"Ah nuts," I say. "Nothing worthwhile."

"Nothing?" Carl asks.

"Not unless you want fruit," I say. "Game?"

"Yeah." Terry reaches for a couple of Aldebbaran oranges. "They're better than nothing."

Deciding he's right, I peel a Saturn mango. They are supposed to be better than the ones grown on Earth. The fruit is sweet and goes a long way to making me feel like I can function.

As soon as we clean up, since Chief Pelham won't let us leave the mess, I search for the Port-A-Sys. It's not where I left it.

"Hoppin' space rocks!" I holler. "Who ripped off my stuff?"

"Slow down," Chief Pelham says. "Where did you leave it?"

"On the sofa," I reply.

"And Angela would have come home for lunch," he says. "Right?"

"Oh, yeah."

No way will I mention how Mom told me to clean up before this too long day got started, and I blew her off. I take off for my bedroom, at the end of a hallway. A deep desire to check the area around the station runs through me, but I can do nothing about it – right now. Living quarters have no outside portholes. In the event of an evacuation, we need as many corridors as possible so the apartments are set in the center of the station. We do have screens that show different views of space or historical sights on Earth.

As soon as I rush into my bedroom, I breathe a sigh of relief. My Port-A-Sys sits right in the middle of my bed, along with a single red chip.

"Uh-oh." I pick up the chip and stuff it in my pocket.

Mom has a system of telling me when I'm getting on her last nerve. She leaves a red chip on whatever I forgot to put away, or near something that needs doing that I ignored. Accumulating five in a week means I can't hang out on the promenade for three days.

Talk about a rough punishment. It's child abuse in my eyes. I'll be stuck in my quarters while my friends hone their skills on the arcade games. It will then take me months to catch up to them.

Carrying the Port-A-Sys under an arm, I return to the other part of the apartment. Chief Pelham has taken over the most comfortable spot, a body-conforming chair in a corner. Terry and Carl sprawl on the floor, our usual place when we gather.

"Did Angela leave you a warning?" Chief Pelham asks.

"Sure did." I hit the floor hard and open the Port-A-Sys. "It's the first in a couple of months. I'll make sure I don't get any others until next week."

"You hope," he says with a smile. "I wouldn't advise upsetting her today. She might hand you the other four all at once."

That image makes me shudder from a very recent memory. I turn on my portable computer and wait for it to boot up.

Five minutes later, I'm still waiting.

"Uh, Terry," I say. "This isn't good."

"Switch." He takes my spot as I roll over by Carl. "You're right," Terry says. "This isn't good. Someone infected your system. Let me guess. You left it on."

"Yeah." I shrug. "So?"

"So, you also left the wireless net on," he says. "That's probably how Jameson rerouted his message through your place."

"Oh."

Looks like I have arrived at the point where I have to keep up on the tech stuff, but no one will ever know. No one except my crew.

"It'll take me a little while to fix this." He shoves a stick into a port.

"I hope I can do it."

His worried tone makes me look at him. He's almost as good as Cassie with computers. Between them, they have never encountered an unsolvable problem. I hope he hasn't run into one now.

"Use the PerSys," he says. "This will take a long time." He looks at Carl. "Too bad you flunked your pilot's test. Sure could use Cassie's help right now."

"Rub it in, why don't you?" Carl jumps to his feet. "Come on, BD. We'll leave him to figure that out and work the 'net."

"Sure."

Thoughts run through my head on how to find out if the person Jameson calls Old One Leg is my dad. Only one thing makes sense, and I need Mom's permission to access the Twelve Stations 'net to find the information. So long as I stay on the Canoples net she doesn't care. Anything else, she wants an adult hanging around.

Big deal. I've seen far worse stuff in school when we studied Life Science. Arguing with her got me five red chips. Hollering unfair right after she gave me the chips earned me another five.

"Chief, can you ask Mom if we can use the 'net?" I ask.

"I'll tell her I watched you." He grins. "Just don't go on a site she won't like."

That will happen because I want information, but he and Mom never need to know. With a wicked grin on my face, I glance at Carl. He returns the grin, and we get to work. Keying up the search engine, I enter pirates, Old One Leg, and space. One hit comes up.

"Whoa!" Carl says under his breath. "Is this what I think it is?"

"Yeah." I explain my suspicions. "We have to do this."

"It's your funeral," he comments. "Don't let me stop you. I've always wanted to know more about pirates."

We troll the site. A couple of times, I stop at a picture to examine it more closely. My suspicions rise each time. On the last link, I release a piercing whistle.

"What?" Chief Pelham moves across the room at astonishing speed.

One minute, he's reclining back with his eyes closed. The next, he pushes Carl and me aside to look at the page.

The face in the pic is so familiar. I see it every day in my mirror. Only this one is older, and I last saw it the day he disappeared.

My dad is alive. He calls himself Old One Leg Bradford in the 24th century now.

CHAPTER TWENTY-TWO

I realize my worst fears while backing away from the PerSys. Dad faked his own death. More than anything, I want to scream it's a lie except for one thing. The pic of him is only a few hours old, according to the time stamp. Now that I know he's alive, I have to find him. He has a lot to explain, beginning with why he left the way he did.

"I need to contact Wade," Chief Pelham says. "He and a couple of the younger men can start trying to have Tom recruit them. We'll use the old double agent scenario to bring these pirates in."

Shocked by his words, I stare at him. Has he lost every brain cell he possesses? Wade and his friends in Security personify law enforcement as much as Chief Pelham does.

"Give me a break!" I yell.

He raises an eyebrow. I remember how his quiet but intense voice put real fear into me when someone else was the target of his anger and gulp a couple of times.

"Uh … not to sound dumb or anything," I say in a much quieter voice, "but don't you think that's a lousy idea."

More than anything, I need this to work. Wade will rush in and announce an arrest in seconds. While I have no desire to protect him, I want a confrontation with Dad to hear why he acted like he did before I slap restraints on him. At the moment, Wade is the only way to accomplish that, unless I can convince everyone to use another Bradford – me.

"Not Wade," I say. "Dad'll never believe he turned traitor."

"You have a point," Carl says. "Heck, Chief, Wade would turn himself in if he forgot to pay for a candy bar."

"That's true." Chief Pelham smiles. "But I don't have a lot of choices. Tom still has a lot of friends in Security."

There is one person in the galaxy Dad will believe turned against Chief Pelham. Most of the station can attest to how much I defended my dad right after his disappearance. That is until Graham and Carson showed up with the wreckage, and then they treated me like an idiot.

Strange emotions surge through me. Most have to do with hunting Dad down and making him pay for his criminal acts. I make a move to leave and run right into the tempered tera-flex like frame of Chief Pelham.

"You won't do it," he says. "I won't risk Angela's anger by letting you get in touch with Tom. This will destroy her enough as it is. She might have wanted a divorce but thinking he was dead hurt her a lot."

Yeah. I know that. Many nights, I heard Mom crying after the official announcement. A couple of times, she swore she would forgive Dad if he would just come back. Of course, she never realized I was standing right outside her bedroom door, ready to comfort her so she stopped crying.

Not that she made a lot of noise. That makes me more determined to protect her.

"Then what?" I ask. "Who can you send? Not Wade or any of his friends. Dad will use them as hostages."

Where am I coming up with this? Joy at the thought of Wade in trouble, the one feeling I'm supposed to have, is the furthest thing from my mind. Too many of my daydreams involve him in hot steam over his head. The most satisfying end to most of those situations is me appearing and hearing him begging me to help him. Of course, I do, but only after making him grovel for a good ten to fifteen minutes. Instead, I want to protect him, and help Security bring my dad in, and then make sure Dad spends the rest of his life cruising around the stars on Fomalhaut, forever forbidden from setting foot on a station.

A beep comes from the combination watch/communicator Chief Pelham wears. At the same time, Wade rushes through the front door.

"One of Wills Adventure Tours shuttles just disappeared," he says, giving me a sympathetic look. "The pilot identified a peculiar flitter following her, and then communications went out. I already sent a rescue team to the last known location."

"How many on the shuttle?" Chief Pelham asks.

Carl and I stare at them open-mouthed. They know who the pilot is. When will they say her name? Is there more they haven't told me?

"It's Cassie," I yell. "Dad has Cassie. Why?"

"Settle down," Wade says. "Where did you get the idea Dad has Cassie? He's dead."

What is he thinking? He's not dumb. I have already explained about Old One Leg Bradford. What will it take to make Wade a believer? Does he need an announcement on Galactic News? Will an expose, going out of the way to make it look like we knew everything all along, force him to face reality?

I won't let that happen. Before we decide how to rescue Cassie, my big brother will accept the truth.

"Dad's alive." I point at the PerSys. "Look at that picture and tell me he isn't."

Before Wade looks, the screen blanks. When the video restores, I see a message in monster purple letters. The darned thing flashes on and off, making it hard to understand what the person wants, until I read the message a couple of times.

I have Cassie Wills.

You have what I want.

Leave it at the place we used to go by ten tonight.

Don't tell anyone about this.

My eyes narrow once the message sinks in. I'm more than ready to take on a person who, as far as I'm concerned, happens to share a name with me. He's no longer any relation to me. Not after what he has done.

"What do they want?" Wade asks. "This doesn't make sense."

Sure, it doesn't make sense. If I'd been like him, that would have been my very first thought. Thank goodness, I'm nothing like my big brother. I know what the message means but have absolutely no plans to give Dad what he wants. Even if I would have given up that particular item.

"What does Tom want, BD?" Chief Pelham asks.

"I have no idea."

Monster lie. When Dad left, he forgot his lucky charm, a piece of eight, a pirate marker from the seventeenth century. Right before the evacuation of Earth, my great-great-great grandpa drilled a hole in the ancient coin and threaded it on a chain. Since then, a male ancestor receives the heirloom on his sixteenth birthday. I took the piece of eight pendant before anyone locked it up not long after we heard Dad died.

I have a way to get Cassie back and make sure he stands trial for his crimes, but only if my buds help. A quick glance at Carl assures me of what I already know. No one hurts his sister without him going after them. Terry gives me a barely perceptible nod when I look at him.

With phase one of the plan complete, I need to come up with a way to fool Wade and Chief Pelham. Problem is I have no idea what to do. They already know my best tricks.

CHAPTER TWENTY-THREE

Wade and Chief Pelham huddle in a corner of the kitchen. I jerk my head at the hallway. A few seconds later, Carl and Terry take off for my bedroom. After snagging some disgusting, drier-than-my-mouth-after-playing-SpaceBall-for-three-hours protein bars, I follow them.

"What's the plan?" Carl asks.

"How do you know I have a plan?" I ask.

"You always have a plan." Terry laughs. "Don't you remember the fake food poisoning attack when we had a pop quiz in Math? Or the day you released a bunch of white mice in Science so no one could use them in the experiment."

"Oh yeah." I grin. "Well, here's all I've come up with. Carl, you need to get a hold of one of your dad's control cards. Just one, I don't care what shuttle it belongs to."

"Not a prob." He flexes a muscle. "I'll even knock over whoever's on your back door and lock them in a closet."

"Good." I nod. "I hadn't thought of that. Go but be quiet." I give him a very serious look. "Be very, very quiet. Wade can hear me hatching trouble across the galaxy."

"Thanks for reminding me." He leaves in a flash, but I can't hear him moving.

With part two of my plan in action, I turn to Terry.

"You have to stay behind," I say. "One of us needs to hack their system and create havoc so the others can slip in. Except for Cassie, you're the only one who can."

"I guess you're right." Terry frowns. "I don't like you and Carl going without someone to watch your back."

"We'll do it for each other," I reassure him. "How far out was Cassie when the trouble call came in?"

Five minutes of work gets him into the communications network. Very illegal, but it's for a great cause.

"She was approaching the first marker," he says. "It pinged her hull, and she reported no problems, but then a couple of minutes later, she sent the SOS."

"I know where they are." I can't help hopping from foot to foot. "You do, too. That place where we went for our science field trip last year." I lean into the hallway to see if Wade or Chief Pelham heard me.

They are nowhere in sight, but I worry about them leaving me alone. Their usual tactic if they think I have a plan to dive into trouble is to stick to me as if I smell like a fresh Venus-mut.

"Give Carl and me thirty minutes," I say. "If you don't hear from us by then, tell Wade and the chief where we went."

"Bring her back, BD," Terry says. "Just bring Cassie back."

"I will."

The words come out with more confidence than I feel. It's only a guess where the pirates have taken her. I start to leave but stop at the door.

"How many people on the shuttle?" I ask.

"Eight," he says. "Why?"

"That lets out a flitter." I give it some thought. "Unless we take two of the expanded models. That'll give us more room. And we won't need a second control card. Carl can slave my ship to his for the takeoff. Once we're away from the station, I won't need to stay connected to him." I nod. "Okay. I'm out of here. Make sure Pelham and Wade don't know I'm gone for half an hour."

Before leaving, I unfasten a clip, pull a very old coin hanging off a chain out of my pocket, and then shove it inside my boot. No way will Dad get his mitts on the piece of eight.

Terry stands straight and salutes me as I slip into the hallway. I wave and creep out the door. Muffled protests from a garbage chute across from my quarters startle me.

"Carl, you didn't," I whisper. "The chief will have us cleaning Jeffries tubes the rest of our lives."

It will be well worth the frustration of being stuck inside a greasy Jeffries tube to have the reassuring thought that no one is coming at us behind our backs. The garbage chutes dump their contents into the skin zone sometime between midnight and three in the morning. As it's not yet two in the afternoon, we have more than enough time to get away from here, and let someone know later where our Security protection is. If, that is, we really want the man or woman figuring out a way to get even for Carl's rather ingenious method of keeping him or her quiet.

"I guess I'd better make sure there isn't a chance someone in Maintenance won't turn on the garbage chute release valve early," I say with a lot of reluctance. "It's only right. Maybe."

A conscience is a terrible thing to have, and an indicator I'm doing what Wade has wanted for years – growing up. After checking, and finding out Carl shoved the officer under the chute instead of in it, I take off to meet him.

He lives one corridor over and fifteen quarters down. I sneak along the steel decking, always watching to make sure no one sees me. For my plan to succeed, we have to get to the SpaceDock without anyone stopping us.

I have barely raised my fist to knock when his door opens. He holds up a control card and smiles. Returning the smile, I nod at the ventilation shaft. His smile dissolves into a look of horror. Carl has a good reason to fear what I silently suggested.

Deck six, where we live, is below deck three, where the SpaceDock is. Instead of sliding down, we have to climb the slippery metal. If someone decides to flush the ventilation system for whatever reason, we can't warn them where we are. Worse, Terry has no way of tracking us in there. Shielding, to keep certain toxins out of the station, makes the whole area a communications dead zone.

Oh, toxins, yeah.

We have to suit up for the trip. Since we aren't on a rescue team, Security, or work at the hospital, we have no suction cups on our boots. Well, we have been in tougher spots. Unfortunately, as I activate my suit, I can't think of when.

The trip up goes in silence. We keep our communicator open on the CI channel, so we can warn each other in case we hear something. Sweat puddles in every joint as I press my back against one side, and use my feet and elbows to make the climb. This is the slowest I have moved in a long time. My estimate of thirty minutes might have been a little optimistic.

Or not.

Fifteen minutes later, we climb into two extended flitters that hold six passengers each and take off. Canoples Control contacts us immediately.

"Unidentified flitters, return to station. No outbound flights by direct order of Chief Pelham," the controller says.

"Not happening." I turn down the volume.

I would have shut off the radio except for a couple of very important reasons. The first is Terry can track our location better if we leave them on. The other? I'm in enough trouble to find myself stuck in my quarters for six months. Turning off the radio will have me grounded the rest of my life. I have a lot of plans, and none of them include listening to Mom yelling at me until I'm older than the stars.

As soon as we leave Canoples Control's visual, I waggle my wings.

Carl's flitter does the same, and I open the ship-to-ship communications.

"Remember where we went for our field trip last year?" I ask.

"Sure," he says. "I'll set course. Stay on my rear."

He zooms off. Pressing the stick forward, I keep him in sight but stay back. No one knows my real plan. Dad has to capture Carl for it to work, since we have to rescue eight innocent people in addition to Cassie and Jan Wilson.

A face appears on the vu-screen in front of me. It's Chief Pelham.

"Come back," he says. "Don't do this, BD."

"Give me time," I say. "Look, I already know Mom will come after me with so many red chips I can't count them. So what? This is personal."

"We can contact Tom and negotiate with him," he says.

"Try," I say, "but you won't convince me to come back. I know what he wants. I have it. He'll get it, but only after he releases Cassie and her passengers."

"BD." His voice holds a warning.

"Nothing you say will make me change my mind. He left it. I think it was by accident. So I'll give it back, but it'll be on my terms."

I shut off everything but ship-to-ship communications. Carl calls a couple of minutes later.

"Terry let me know that Pelham found out we left," Carl says.

"I already know," I say. "Pelham contacted me. We're in deep now. If you want to go back, so you're not in trouble, I'll understand."

I hate what I'm saying, but I have to give him a way to bow out of this mad plan gracefully.

"We're twins," he says. "I can feel how scared she is. I'm going."

Like I expect any other answer. Whenever I decide to take the situation into my hands, to ignore orders from Security and Mom, I always give my buds the chance to back off. None of them ever have.

We fly through Jupiter's outer rings. I press the comm button.

"Carl, don't hate me for this," I say.

"What?"

"I need you captured," I say. "Cassie and her passengers have to understand the plan so they don't mess it up for us."

I outline my idea, and he agrees almost as soon as I stop talking.

"Don't do anything I wouldn't," I say.

"Gotcha."

He sweeps left and takes off at high speed. I say a prayer. Not that we attend church at the station, everyone does their own thing when it comes to worship. Right about now, I want the full service with a minister shouting halleluiah, like in our history-vids. A great huge cathedral, the choir dressed in red and purple robes swaying from side to side, a preacher prancing the center aisle, the congregation hollering "Amen, brother!" at the man's every word will give me just the tiniest bit of confidence that we'll succeed.

A flitter races out of the clouds steaming up from the planet. Not Dad's, but the ship looks just as fearsome. Painted purple scales cover the spacecraft's skin, and it has a snarling mouth on the cockpit area.

What makes it so scary is the way the pilot matches Carl move for move.

"Don't fight," I whisper into the open mic.

"I won't," Carl says. "See you on the flipside, buddy."

Laser blasts lance the air. One hits his tail. Smoke pours out of the engine compartment and the flitter spins so fast I begin to fear for his safety. He spirals toward the planet.

CHAPTER TWENTY-FOUR

Carl's flitter disappears from sight. One minute, he's in front of me and the next, I'm alone in space just off Jupiter. The aloneness hits me the hardest. Living on a space station means you have people around you all the time. There's never a chance to be alone.

Seconds later, the possible loss of one of my best buds slams into my gut like a fist I didn't see. My plan may have caused his death, and there's no way to check to see if he's okay. Any attempt to contact him might endanger our mission. He wouldn't want me to put Cassie in more danger, making my decision to ignore him and get on with the job at hand even more difficult. But not without something I haven't done in years. Tears make my eyes itch; tears of rage for how all this came about – Dad's selfishness and reckless attitude about anything not concerning himself.

"No." I won't let the pirates get away with this. After turning the radio back on, I key the mic.

"They shot Carl down," I say. "It wasn't Dad, but I bet it was someone working for him."

A quiet crackle is all I hear for a couple of seconds, and then the light touch of someone keying their mic.

"We're on our way," Chief Pelham says. "Don't try to do this yourself. Let us take care of Tom and his people."

That will be far too easy. Dad owes me a big explanation, and I want to be the first one to confront him.

"Terry knows where we are," I say. "You'll have to get the coordinates from him. I'm going silent now."

Chief Pelham and the rescue team have no reason to know I plan to switch frequencies instead, in an effort to find the pirate's channel. The change goes well, but my vision keeps blurring with tears. No matter what frequency I scan, no one is talking. I even try to call out to Dad, using his name, Tom Bradford, but the crackle of an unanswered radio is the only response.

If I were a pirate – not that it will ever happen – I sure would want to talk to the guy holding what I want. These fools are beyond stupid, making them far more dangerous than anyone realizes. Stupid guys tend to lash out and destroy anything around them.

Will the lack of a response from the pirates stop me? *Wrong!* That only makes me more determined to bring them to justice. I followed Carl's spiraling descent, after his attacker vanishes from sight.

"I'm coming," I say to the canopy as I fight my way through Jupiter's atmosphere. "Don't give up. We may still have a chance."

The planet below me has very few safe landing spots. I only know of one and have no idea how to work the ship's computer to find another. The piece of eight slides around inside my boot, distracting me when I need to find a parking beacon.

"Where are you?" I mutter under my breath.

Oh, like worrying about someone hearing me is important. *So not!* I developed the habit after Mom discovered us practicing to go down the girders in the skin area. I had moved aside the ceiling tiles in my bedroom and was swinging from one to another. My bed provided the perfect landing spot when we missed a catch. Carl and I crashed into each other, making enough noise for everyone on the promenade, nine levels above us, to wonder what happened. She rushed into the bedroom. Her quiet but intense lecture stung a little less than the ultimate punishment. The red chips started appearing that night.

"Sure wish I was back with that first red chip right now," I say. "Heck, it'd be worth it if Mom handed me a million red chips if I could just see Carl's face and know he's okay."

While looking for a place to land, I hope today turns out better than that one so long ago. Back then, we still had to learn about sneaking around and staying quiet.

"Where did you crash, Carl?"

Scanning the area, I catch sight of a crooked flitter tail in the mists and fog. A closer look proves it's my quarry. I flip a switch next to the control yoke and angle toward the spacecraft, hoping against hope he's still around.

After a glance at my chronometer, I can't believe my eyes. I have wasted almost an hour searching. It sure hasn't seemed like that long. By now, Chief Pelham and the officers he detailed to come after us will be very close to if not tracking my every move.

I have to do my thing and get the hostages back on their way to safety. Then I can put the next part of my plan into motion. Only one little glitch exists. Carl, because of the threat to Cassie, will insist on staying with me.

"Telling him he has to protect them until they meet up with Security won't work." I set the landing sequence into motion. "I'll just have to insult him into leaving."

While the ship's automated controls take over the most dangerous part of my mission, I go over what I can use to insult Carl enough so he'll leave. Nothing I think of works. He's like me, insult proof until someone uses what we dubbed "the deadlies" a year ago. Those include stuff like making fun of our business or family. Not important to most teens, but to us the biggest things we live for. We also agreed never to use such ammunition against each other.

"Until now," I whisper.

The landing skids contact the pad designed to keep visitor parking away from the planet's protected areas. I breathe a sigh of relief. Carl isn't the only person to fail his flying test, and we both did it during the most important part – landings. Even though most ships have automated systems, Twelve Stations Driving Control requires everyone to park without setting off an alarm before issuing a license.

For some reason, girls do it without thinking. Guys, on the other hand, take two or three tries to get it right.

"I hate this part," I mumble. "Darn, I really hate these suits."

Jupiter, while beautiful and full of wondrous sights, can't support human life. I activate my gear and pop the hatch. After securing the ship, I run over to check his. No sign of him but not unexpected since he failed to communicate. I smile when I notice how his landing beacon blinks in a code we developed during our second year of operation.

"Gotcha." I grin and think back to how hard it was to learn how to program a flitter to accept this series of blinks. One thing I know for sure. Carl's okay. "Thanks, buddy."

I lift the hatch right inside the airlock and discover video of the pirates who took my best bud hostage. None of the men are Dad, but of them all have at one time or another worked for Security. He fired all of them for various offenses right before he disappeared.

Then comes the biggest surprise of all, and I have no way to notify Chief Pelham. While Carl struggles with his captors, Carson and Graham stroll onto the ship.

Tinny voices erupt from the speakers. I set the sound to the lowest level.

"You!" Carl lunges at the pair and knocks them over. "Where's my sister?"

"All wrapped up nice and tight." Graham ties up Carl. "What happened to Bradford? We expected him to chase the girl."

"Don't know." He stares right at the camera. "Shouldn't you go back to Security and shuffle micro-chips?"

"I quit." Carson grabs Carl's hair and yanks his head back. "Where's Bradford?"

"Didn't come." His ever-widening smile looks fierce. "No one knows I left. I came after my sister."

I want to dance for joy when the traitors believe him but only part of me. The other part works on autopilot as I move to the console and remove the control card. After sealing the card into a pocket, I check the flitter.

This ship will never fly again. Mine won't without the control card. The time I take to secure that card ensures the pirates have no more ships.

"This is a lot bigger than I figured." I step onto the ramp and scan the parking area. Nothing in sight. "Pelham will skin me alive for not waiting, but I don't have a choice."

Dad's choice of his primary hostage forces my decision. Anyone with half a brain knows how I feel about Cassie, and have since we tumbled in the kindergarten play area. She always teases me to push my limits, and I do it just so a girl won't do better than me. I'm not sure when that changed to this protective, jealous space-ghoul roaring in my heart, but I'll do anything to get her away from my dad.

My booted feet slam into the ramp as I take off in the direction the pirates did. I have to depend on Carl's ingenuity to find the trail, and hope his captors haven't knocked him out.

Before losing sight of the landing pad, I locate my first clue. It's not much and a Canoples cred could have come from anyone. As I examine the coin closely, I smile. This particular cred is from Rendall! Other than Governor Jackson's group, only Carl, Terry, and I have them. Governor Jackson is too dumb to be behind the pirates, and the rest of his group follow his orders even it if means going to detention. That leaves them out. Since Terry is safe back on the station, I know Carl has shown me the way.

Keeping my eyes peeled on the ground, with a quick peek in all directions every few steps so no one surprises me; I find the next cred without a problem. Thank goodness I did. The path splits in three directions. I almost missed the correct turn because I was about to go left instead of down the center.

The sound of spacecraft engines whining as they pass overhead makes me move faster, take more chances, ignore the little voice in my head screaming at me to slow down. I have to find everyone before Security arrives.

Mist swirls around me. It thickens until I almost have to crawl to find the next four creds. A dark mound rises up in from of my face. I stop and feel it. Voices come from inside what appears to be a cave.

"Where's BD?"

Fury and fear fight for domination within me. I know that voice!

CHAPTER TWENTY-FIVE

My suspicions now a certainty, I move closer to the cave entrance and go over all the plans whirling through my mind. Everything keeps coming back to one problem, no matter how badly Dad treated us, I still want to rush in and hug him.

No way! He won't get off that easy. Everything is far too serious at this point to forgive him.

"Okay, Carl," I whisper. "Hang on for another minute or two."

I take a couple of deep breaths and listen closely to the ongoing conversation. Dad keeps yelling at Carl to tell him where I am. I move with extreme caution toward them. Finally, after five long years, I have the chance to tell Dad what I think about his actions. First, though, I have to make sure eleven people are on their way back to Canoples. The piece of eight now under my toes is my bargaining chip.

Sure hope this plan works.

"Tell me where BD is," he shouts. "I won't ask again."

They aren't far into the cave. A snicker works its way up my throat. My buds aren't afraid of much but our fears are normal – a pop quiz, our parents finding out about our outrageous plans, missing a meal.

What I hear from my dad, the traitor who let me think he died a hero's death, is abject fear.

All those ghost stories he told me when I was a little kid seem to have upset him. They never scared me, but he always acted as if he believed them.

Puh-leeze! Anyone with half a brain knows there are no such things as Jupiter Man-Monsters.

"I swear I don't know," Carl says in a weak voice. "I came after my sister and her passengers. Where are they?"

Thanks, buddy! My thought gives me a few minutes to get rid of the hug Dad urge. No one talks to my buds like that!

I peek around a corner and catch Carl's attention. He nods at another tunnel, one with twenty or thirty men between it and me. I've done tougher stuff. Give me a couple of minutes as soon as I'm out of this situation and I'll try to remember them, except one.

I paid for that stunt. My ears still ring from Mom's scolding. Then she hugged me so hard that she almost broke a couple of ribs.

Mom won't hug me if I don't bring Carl and Cassie home. An image of millions of red chips raining down on me as she goes off worse than she ever has brings a shiver. *She'll never stop yelling.*

I have to make it to that tunnel and rescue the hostages. Carl looks fine, except for a black eye and no protective gear. That must be why he sounds weak. Before I take off to rescue Cassie and her passengers, I need to find a way to make Dad have Carl put on his gear.

An idea forms. I can work on Dad's fears. He collected a motley bunch of men, and they all have the same weakness. They actually believe the children's stories they used to scare us.

They are about to find out there is some truth to those tales. My truth!

My search for something on my suit that will help takes forever. I finally lock my attention on an item I've never used. No time like the present, and it's the perfect device to lend truth to my fairy tale.

"Hope this works," I whisper.

Using my right thumb to activate the controls, I wait until a projection unit illuminates. Then I enter what I hope are the right parameters and step away from the wall. I hold my arms in front of me and rock from side to side while walking toward the men. After pursing my lips, and opening an exterior speaker, I moan loudly.

"What's that?" someone yells.

Other cries follow, most of them full of fear. The sound of footsteps running away brings relief, and a lot of laughter. Those stupid men ran away from a seventeen-year-old! They worked Security at one time or another, but all it takes to put a serious scare into them is some bad acting. None of them even bothers to investigate to find out what made the noise.

After another peek, I breathe a sigh of relief. Carl's alone. I run over to him and activate his gear.

"Thanks," he says. "Get Cass out of here."

"Not without you," I say. "How far away is she?"

It's good to see him in fighting form. He manages a weak grin and makes sure the seals on his suit are tight.

"Not sure." He struggles to his feet. "Dad'll slaughter me! They wrecked my flitter."

His dad will probably slaughter both of us, but we'll promise to give over our share of any future cases until we pay for the flitter's repair. Unless Chief Pelham hands out a reward for this episode, and we can use it for the repairs. The prospect of extra creds sounds good, but I move away from the opportunity and lock onto the rest of our mission.

"I saw." I take Carl's arm and lead him into the cave he indicated. "We have bigger worries than your dad. Pelham should have landed by now. We don't have much time."

"Then put some moves into it." He shoves in front of me. "We need to get Cass out of here. Your dad didn't plan to let her or her passengers go."

That burns right through me. Dad has acted like most pirates from history, without honor. I plan to make things right real soon.

Carl and I hurry into the cave. It's small and smells like sulfur. There sure must be a lot of the element for it to penetrate the suit's defenses. We locate the hostages, and I grin. Cassie grins back. My gal never sits around waiting for someone else to fix a mess. She has her passengers lined up behind her. All of them wear their protective gear. I indicate the main cave behind me.

"Get to your shuttle and take them back to the station," I say.

She points in the other direction.

"That's where they made me park," she says.

Her voice sounds so sweet. To keep from making a fool of myself in front of everyone else, I settle for counting her passengers instead of hugging her. There is one more than I expected.

"Who's the other person?" I step back in case he is part of Dad's pirate gang.

"Security," she says. "I tried to tell those jerks he was a passenger, but they didn't believe me."

I take a closer look and identify him as Jan Wilson through the faceplate, but it's an almost impossible identification to make. He has two black eyes and blood dribbles from a split lip. He reaches out to balance against the wall when his knees give out.

"Better have a couple of the men help him walk," I say. "He looks like someone beat him up. Who?"

Like I have a lot of experience seeing people who have been beat up. The only time I have ever seen it happened was eight hours ago, after Security found Missy's parents. Will this day never end?

"Your dad," Cassie says. "He remembered him as Wade's best friend from school. You." She points at two passengers near him. "Help Jan walk to the shuttle."

"Go with her." I glance at Carl. "I'll bring back my flitter. Don't explain to your dad until I return. We'll figure out how to pay for yours."

"I'm staying." He sounds determined.

"Cassie will need help." I want him to stay, but my wishes doesn't matter. "Make sure Jan is all right."

"Hoppin' space rocks!" His voice explodes in my ear. "You can't do this alone."

I touch his arm. "Sure I can. Besides, I'm not alone. Chief Pelham should be here soon. All I'll do is stall."

Carl looks ready to argue again, and I get ready for one of our push and shove fights. Cassie can't go alone. She needs him so she can concentrate on getting back to the station.

"You two don't need to get all guy on me." She laughs. "I've handled this so far. Let Carl stay if he wants.

"I need him with you." I glance at my gal. "Don't argue, Cass. Dad never wanted to release you."

"Right." Her laughter gets louder. "Like that had a chance of happening."

The sound is so good I can't help joining in with her. We stop when someone runs toward us.

"Take off," I whisper. "Don't stop no matter what you hear."

CHAPTER TWENTY-SIX

Everyone freezes in place. Not even the sound of someone taking a breath breaks the silence.

We stare in the direction of the footsteps. They stop. A screeching movement makes me tense. If I have to, I'll tackle whoever it is to give the others a chance to get away.

"Found it," Graham yells.

His squeaky voice echoes off the stone walls and then becomes muffled. I cock my head to figure out why the differences and work up the nerve to take a peek around the corner. Of course, I can't stick my head around the corner so I use a little mirror that comes out of my helmet on a mechanical arm. Seconds later, I see him adjusting his facemask. He keeps lifting the visor up and down.

"It was right where you left it, Old One Leg," he yells, lifting the facemask again. "Be right back."

A low growl works its way up my throat. I swallow hard to keep the threatening sound from leaking out. Seconds later, he runs toward another part of the cave. After his footsteps fade, I turn to the hostages.

"Go now," I order.

I move away from my buds and wait for the hostages to disappear from sight. Jan pauses despite his injuries, until I shake my head and point at the rear of the escaping hostages.

"Pelham was about ten minutes behind me with a full team," I say. "Protect Cassie, Carl, and the passengers. That's your job."

He must have believed me because he limps after the hostages without arguing. The passengers Cassie told to help him reach for his arms. He shrugs them off and stumbles out of the cave.

"Are you sure about this?" Carl stands by the passageway entrance. "I can stay if you need help."

"Go," I tell him. "I have this under control. Make sure no one stops Cass from getting away from here."

He waits for another second, enough time to make me think about using one of "the deadlies" on him. Then he races after the hostages. That's good because I can't prove Pelham has a team, or they're right behind me. I sure hope so because with everyone safe, I have no idea what to do next.

One thing I know with absolute certainty. I won't give up the piece of eight inside my boot. Dad can yell, scream, and threaten all he wants. That old coin is mine. He lost all rights to it when he decided to live as an outlaw.

When I no longer hear the hostages, I go on a search for the biggest traitor of all. Dad gave up a great life to follow his ancestor's footsteps. The way I see it, he did the wrong thing. Taking the easy path and ripping people off for what he wants sure gives him nice stuff, but it also makes his actions worse. Especially since he always treated criminals like scum. Not once do I remember him ever giving a lawbreaker a second chance. He always made sure anyone he caught breaking the law spent a long time on Fomalhaut. He used to tell me a person was only as good as their reputation, and I believed him.

I will keep believing my reputation is what makes me good. My choices will never let me give him a chance to get away. I take off on a desperate search for the man so willing to throw away his family.

Watch out, you lousy pirates. A smile forms on my face. BD Bradford is going to put you on Fomalhaut for the rest of your lives.

There must have been a hundred small caves off the main one. I investigate about half, and avoid Pelham and his team when I hear them calling me. I even turn off my communicator so I don't accidentally give away my location.

This is important. No one can tell me about it later. I have to confront Dad, and let him know that I'm not the kid he trained to follow in his footsteps. Then I will gladly accept whatever punishment Mom gives me.

Well, almost any punishment. My smile disappears as I imagine all those red chips with my name on them. Mom will understand. I hope. She can't ground me for the rest of my natural life. Can she?

The pirates huddle in the center of the last cave I encounter. I have to push through a negative pressure field to reach them. Dad looks at me. For a split-second, his eyes widen in surprise and, then, he appears as if he's relieved I found him.

"You don't need gear in here," he says.

"Really?" I make no move to remove my gear. "Is that another lie? Like all the other lies you told me about honor and truth?"

Low blow, but I don't feel charitable. He looks like ten million miles of bad space lanes. The deep black hair, so black it has blue highlights, plasters against his skull from fear sweat. His eyes dart from side to side in an effort to see everything at once.

"It's not what you think," he says.

Oh, he expects me to believe him. I have a news flash. Dad blew it with me. I will never believe what he has to say again.

"Sure it is." I fold my arms over my chest. "You ran away and decided to rip people off. Do you sell space dust, too?"

"I need to make a living."

His weak, pathetic excuse erases all sympathy I might have for him. Space dust pickles the brains of the idiots stupid enough to use it. Anyone making it risks death because of how easily the labs blow up. Even worse, they endanger everyone around them. A space dust lab blowing up causes explosive decompression on a station. Bulkheads can only protect the people outside the affected area. Not many cookers go down to a planet to make their junk. They avoid the chance Security will catch them when they return with their product.

"Why Cassie?" I ask in an effort to distract him.

"I knew you'd come after her," he says. "Did you bring the medallion?"

"Nope."

I never break eye contact. First rule of lying, act like I'm telling the truth. That never works with Mom, but I figure he can't tell a lie from the truth.

"I need that coin. It's my good luck charm," he says. "Get it and return here in less than an hour, or I'll hurt your girlfriend."

A chuckle bursts out of me. "Did you really think I'd confront you without making sure Cassie and her passengers aren't safe? That I'd come alone? Pelham's right behind me."

Moving my right thumb, I open my communicator and find Security's channel. Chatter in the background indicates the search is close.

"Sorry, Dad, you'll have to do better than that," I say. "Cassie, Carl, and everyone else are on their way back to the station."

"Hold on." Wade's tinny voice echoes in my ear.

"BD turned his communicator back on. Rayson, track him now."

Relief floods through me. Sometimes, going with my gut feeling turns out good. With Security on their way, I let fearlessness take over.

"I can get on and off the station without anyone knowing I'm there," Dad says. "I'll come when you least expect it. You'll spend the rest of your life looking over your shoulder."

The piece of eight medallion he wants so desperately bunches up under my little toe. It hurts, but I endure the pain so he won't know I brought it.

"Oh, I'm so scared," I say in my best I-don't-care-voice. "Not!"

"Search him," he orders, waving a couple of his men forward. "Strip the brat if you have to, but find that medallion."

I have to do something fast. No way will I let him have the medallion so he can justify his existence as the current Old One Leg Bradford. My gaze drops to where he stands on both legs, neither of which looks like a cybernetic replacement.

"Ya know." I grin and listen to the Security chatter in my ear. They're even closer than I thought. "If you're gonna take on a nickname, you really should use one that fits you. Have you thought of Big-Fat-Coward Bradford or I-Abandoned-My-Family-to-Act-Like-a-Jerk Bradford?" I laugh. "I have it. Terminally-Stupid Bradford. It's the perfect name for a space pirate."

Dad's face turns purple, the same shade as a Martian banana right before it turns rotten. When I was a little kid, that would have scared the life out of me, but I feel nothing. Sure I'm his son, but in looks only. I listened to his words, ones I know now are false, and I took those words to heart. Faced with what he has become, I make a decision.

He no longer has the power to tell me what to do.

"Wade," I yell. "Last cave off the right passage. His whole crew is here, including Carson and Graham."

The last bit I add as a warning to Chief Pelham. His problem in Security has revealed itself without creating a scandal.

"You just had to blow it," Dad says.

The threatening tone of his voice scares me. My head jerks up before I can react any other way. He pulls a blaster from a hip holster. I gulp. That is the biggest, blackest blaster I have ever seen.

CHAPTER TWENTY-SEVEN

Fear might have locked my muscles, if I let it. I can always wait for rescue, but steel makes up my nerves, and there is no back up in me. Gulping back the abject horror running through me at the thought of Dad's threat to use the blaster, I slide a foot backward.

"Don't move," he says.

"You don't get to tell me what to do anymore." My voice shakes. *Not good.* I swallow hard and try again. "You're dead. Did you forget that little detail? Dead people can't tell the living what to do."

Talk about a desperate move. I just goofed up big time. He grins, and I know I only have seconds to stop him.

"Did it feel good to hurt Mom?" I ask. "Are you proud of making her cry because you died?"

Power fills me when he looks like he cares. But not for long, his worried expression disappears in about a quarter of a second.

"She threw me out," he says. "Happened the day I disappeared. I know it didn't bother Angela to hear that I died. She probably celebrated with a party."

This is news. One thing has to change, my family needs to share important information. Will it take this jerk standing in front of me holding a blaster to make my mom and brother understand I'm not a kid anymore? Before I make things even worse by telling Dad he's a total loser, static crackles in my ear.

"Don't make Tom mad," Chief Pelham says. "Use anything but Angela. He hadn't cared about her for a long time, even though she still loved him when she told him to leave."

Not the time to learn that tidbit, but I understand why. Tearing my gaze from the blaster, I stare at Dad.

"I can't believe you'd shoot me," I say, stalling for time. "Even you aren't stupid enough to think you'll escape."

Groans burst through the communicator's earpiece. Okay, maybe Pelham and the Security team will learn to give me better clues about handling Dad. No one has been really forthcoming about this side of him.

"Tone it down," Wade says. "You can't upset Dad. He really doesn't care about us."

Now he wants to share information. If I knew this sooner, I might have had a chance to stop Dad from causing problems.

"You always did have a mouth on you, Bradley," Dad says, grinning as he activates the blaster. "I'm about to fix that mouth."

"Don't call me Bradley," I say. "I hate that name. Can't you get anything right?"

More groans sound through my earpiece. The Security team sounds like a bunch of Martian cows near milking time.

Gross!

Dad's eyes narrow until his face scrunches up.

"I gave you that name," he says. "You'll use it, for as much time as you have left."

A loud, annoying whine fills the cavern. Time to beat feet or figure out what else I can do to stop what I'm sure will be a rather painful experience. Taking a blaster shot isn't on my things-to-do list, and Mom will probably rip off my head for letting it happen.

The thunder of footsteps approaches. It's time for me to get out of the line of fire and make like a good citizen of the Twelve Stations. My decision firms when I also hear the screaming sound of a shuttle's engine making a full throttle takeoff.

"That's Cassie," I say. "She's pretty good at those fast takeoffs, isn't she?"

To my everlasting relief, all those pirates look at the rock ceiling. Combined, none of them has the intelligence of a Uranus monkey, and those creatures are nothing more than annoying pains in the backside who steal food right off the nearest plate. I push back through the negative pressure field, thanking my lucky stars I haven't removed my gear, and run right into Chief Pelham and Wade.

"Back there." I point at the chamber. "Try acting like a Jupiter Man-Monster. They really believe those fairy tales."

"Stay with BD, Wade," the chief says with a chuckle. "We'll clean up the mess."

With the situation under control, my knees weaken. Why I don't know, but I have to lean against a wall, or I'll fall over. Wade gets up in my face as soon as I slump against the uneven rock.

"That was about the stupidest stunt you've ever pulled," he says.

His words sound so good I hold back my usual snappy reply. All I can do is watch with satisfaction as Chief Pelham and his men take Dad and the pirates into custody. After the pirate gang suits up and has restraints fastened around their wrists, ankles, and someone chains them together, I straighten.

No way will I let those losers think they scared me right down to my toes. I still shake but have the problem mostly under control.

"Tell me I heard Cassie and Carl getting away," I say in a low voice.

"They did," Wade says. "I didn't get the whole story, but Carl insisted you stayed to protect them. BD, I don't know if I should congratulate you or scream until your ears ring. What you did was really brave. I don't know if I could have done it."

"Sure you would have," I say. "Can you congratulate me and leave the screaming to Mom? She'll do enough for everyone."

He smiles. "Yeah. Congrats. You did the right thing."

Chief Pelham walks through the negative pressure field, followed by the prisoners and other Security officers. I concentrate on Dad.

He no longer looks scary. It's pretty hard to intimidate anyone with wrists and ankles shackled and a chain connecting him to his gang. I smile in his direction.

"I did have that piece of eight," I say. "But I would have never given it to you. Old One Leg Bradford, the real pirate, did good. You forgot that, didn't you, Dad? Old One Leg never stole money for his own pleasure."

"He was a fool," Dad says. "Creds make the galaxy turn."

"Creds are nice." I move closer to Wade. "Family is better. You threw yours away."

The last I see of him, Dad spits at me. Laughter bubbles out. He sure looks funny with a big blob of spit inside his helmet.

"Let's get you out of here," Wade says, glaring at Dad. "You don't need to listen to him."

"Can I get a snack first?" I ask. "I'm–"

"Starving," Wade says. "You'll have to wait until we're back on the station. We're not equipped for the biggest black hole in the galaxy."

"Hey!" I protest. "I'm not the biggest black hole in the galaxy." I grin. "Maybe the second biggest. I'm a growing kid. I need my energy."

"Yeah. Sure." He walks beside me back to where I parked the ship. "Give me the control card."

The trip back to Canoples passes in silence. He pilots the flitter since, as he puts it, I still have to pass my piloting test. Like he needs to remind me. The thought of failing something as simple as a landing burns through me every time I think about the humiliating moment.

When we reach the station, he parks as easily as he does everything else. Rubbing my face in the steel decking will feel better. That's Wade. He has to show off about everything.

"Well." He looks at me, a grin spreading from ear to ear. "Ready?"

"Never." I unlatch my restraints. "But why wait? Mom'll probably ground me for the rest of my life." I shrug. "Not that I really have anything to do with the promenade messed up."

We walked into the SpaceDock. There she is, right in front of us, one foot tapping furiously, her fists curled against her hips. The vision of millions of red chips cascading over me returns, only this time it's worse – there are zillions and zillions of those things.

"How's it going?" I ask

Wrong thing to say. Mom starts in on me right away.

"How dare you?" she screams. My mom, the pediatric nurse, stands all of five feet three inches tall. Five feet, three inches of pure terrorist as far as I'm concerned. Her brown hair, heart-shaped face, and light blue eyes mirror Wade's, but on her it looks better. Right now, she has the fiercest expression I have ever seen.

I almost open my mouth to lodge my obligatory protest, until I notice she has her attention focused on the prisoners walking off the Security shuttle. Dad leads them.

"Ah, shut up, Angela," he says.

"Bad," I say in a very low voice so she doesn't hear me. "Very bad. No one tells Mom to shut up. That only makes her yell louder."

"Not at all the way to handle Mom," Wade says in an equally low voice.

We glance at each other, and our grins grow. He and I lean against a wall to enjoy the show. Chief Pelham takes up a position on my other side.

"This will be good," the chief says. "Tom should know better."

All of us struggle not to laugh. As one, we cover the lower part of our faces with a hand. Mom upset can and will take on anyone she thinks is mocking her.

"Don't you dare tell me to shut up," she yells. "You took off, abandoned your sons, and never once thought about the damage you did to them. Don't worry about staying married to me, Tom. As soon as I find the right adjudicator, I'll divorce you!"

"I told you to shut up," Dad says. "Why don't you ever do what I want?"

"Me! Me?" She sputters. "You let us think you died." She begins to laugh. "This will be so easy. You blew it, Tom."

"Huh?" His jaw drops open, and he looks like someone punched him.

I elbow Wade. My big brother snickers.

"She's right," Chief Pelham says. "Tom let everyone think he died. Angela just has to file for an immediate dissolution at the court."

"So that means they aren't married?" I ask.

"Not since the day Dad made everyone think he died," Wade says. "He'll have to answer fraud charges for that stunt."

We start laughing. I mean the real laugh that comes deep in the gut. Mom glances in our direction, and I gulp.

Oh yeah. She's about to dump a whole bunch of red chips on me.

"Yeah." She returns her attention to Dad. "You committed fraud, Tom. Enjoy the rest of your life – on Fomalhaut."

She goes back into the station without saying a word to me.

"Wow!" I say. "Do you think she'll forget I took off without permission, broke about a thousand rules, and almost got killed?"

"Don't push it." Chief Pelham smiles. "Why don't you go home, and let her work off a little more steam?"

"Sure." I grin. "Too bad the promenade is all torn up. I sure could use a piping hot Gut-Buster. Don't get me wrong. The frozen ones were okay, but I need a fresh one."

"Go home," he says. "I'll make sure the promenade is repaired first. Think of it as a reward."

I have one thing to do first – find my buds. They're right outside the bulkhead. Carl, Cassie, and Terry wear smiles larger than mine. As we start to walk back into the station, with nothing more on our minds than finding a snack, Mom appears from around a corner. My heart starts thumping loud and hard.

"There you are, don't think this is over. No red chips, this time." She says with a forced smile. "The judge made time for me, so I have two minutes to get to the courtroom. You, home, right now. Eat dinner... a healthy one and clean up... everything."

"Sure."

She starts to walk away but stops and looks at me again. Sweat streams from my every pore.

What did I do now?

"I want you to move Wade's stuff into your room," she says. "Missy is staying with us until her parents are released from the hospital. You're responsible for babysitting her."

"Aw, Mom!" I holler. "She's a little kid!"

I'm talking to her back. Unwilling to test how far I can take her goodwill, I race over to a lift and stab the actuator. The rest of my buds join me, and we take off on a totally new adventure for Canoples Investigations, cleaning.

The enforced babysitting isn't new, but I dread the amount of time Missy will have to come up with more BD Bradford stories.

CHAPTER TWENTY-EIGHT

Six months go by in a blur. I had my eighteenth birthday not long after I helped arrest Dad. I'm now an adult, but I still have problems figuring out when everyone will accept that. High school finishes for me in a huge way, with one big scare about three weeks before graduation.

We find out we have to learn tech-geek to pass the graduation test. Cassie tutors me so I manage to get enough answers right but forget most of the weird language the second I leave the classroom. In the last hour, I've not only finished school, but also done so well that Mom can't complain about my grades. Cassie got top honors, but Carl, Terry, and I aren't that far behind her. My future stretches before me, but there are a few things to finish first.

Graduation happens tomorrow morning. It's a huge thing on Canoples, especially since I became a hero after capturing the space pirates. Galactic News and Inside Galaxy want to interview me after the ceremony. I told them no. No way will I tell the galaxy about my dad, a man who terrorized everyone on the station to make a cred.

In two minutes, I plan to show Rendall who has the better amateur SpaceBall team. Carl, Terry, Mick Anglin, and Jack Simpson stand beside me. We wear silver shorts and royal blue shirts with Canoples Pirates emblazoned across our chests. The team uniform even has a survival suit built in, making them far bulkier than we are. We used to be the Canoples Space Ghouls. My idea to change the name came after the other stations gave us a hard time about the pirates.

"Gear up," Mick says.

He's the captain, and the best SpaceBall player in history. The station's professional team has already asked him to skip college and play for them. Mick said no, he wants a degree in volcanology. He loves watching volcanoes erupt and can't wait for Io to do its thing.

We strap on elbow and kneepads, fasten helmet straps, and adjust anti-grav belts. Once ready, we wait for the whistle.

"Make it good." Mick takes a step after a whistle echoes through the stadium. "Let's show everyone why we got this far."

The crowd claps when we move into the stadium. I wave at Wade, Mom, and Chief Pelham. The chief is my step-dad now, and I love it. Cassie leads cheers on the deck below where we'll soon play. Now that I know how hard she works with her team to pump up the crowd, I no longer give her a hard time about doing girl things. Besides, she looks really cute in her cheerleader uniform of shorts and a tank top.

"I don't believe it," Terry says.

"What?" I tear my gaze from the prettiest girl in the galaxy, and my jaw ends up somewhere near my knees. "Is this a joke?"

"Nope." Carl groans.

Mick and Jack roll their eyes but stay quiet. None of us can stop what's about to happen.

Governor Jackson and his wife prance across the deck from the Rendall side of the court. From our side, Governor Tulane, his wife, and Lisa wave at spectators while walking to meet them. The whole weird scene looks like three Saturn elephants overwhelming two Martian beanpoles.

To my relief, Cassie and the rest of the cheerleaders abandon the playing field fast. The governors meet and shake hands under the center of the SpaceBall court.

"My boys will repeat what they did the last time our teams met in a championship game. We are, after all, the reigning galactic champs for the last eight years," Governor Jackson says and launches into a speech.

So he thinks I've forgotten all about that game eight years ago. I may have been a kid then, but I'll never forget the humiliation at Rendall's hands. Oh no, I'll never forget, and I have just the move today that'll make sure Canoples wins – and it'll all be legal!

"Wanna bet?" I mumble.

"They're pretty good," Mick says.

"We have a reason to beat them," I say.

The team gathers in a huddle, and I explain the re-kat incident leading to the longest day of my life.

"BD's right," Jack, the goaltender, says. "We'll go all out but keep it clean. I don't want anyone saying we cheated."

"Got that straight," I say.

We break the huddle and wait for Governor Tulane to respond. He's almost as boring.

"But today isn't about politics," he says after making the usual "my team is better than your team" comments. "It's time for Canoples to end Rendall's championship reign."

To roaring cheers, the five of us activate our anti-grav belts. Mick meets Rendall's captain in center court. The ball drops from the ceiling.

Mick's hand moves so fast it's a blur. He slams a fist into the ball, and it soars across the court right in my direction. I lift a foot and deliver a kick that sends it to Terry, who passes it to Carl. He shoots it right past Rendall's goal tender.

First score! We have the advantage and press it throughout the game. For every two points we score, Rendall only picks up one. With minutes left, in danger of losing our lead from a concerted push by them, I see my opportunity for the special move I've practiced for just this moment.

The ball flies in my direction after a bad kick from their center. Unless I jet over there, it will miss me by a couple of feet. Flipping backward, keeping one foot outstretched with the other tucked behind the opposite knee, I kick and then punch the ball toward Terry. He passes to Mick, who sends it toward Carl. Seconds later, after a flying toss from Carl, the ball smacks the center of Rendall's goal. The ref indicates another score as the final whistle blows.

Roars and cheers soar around us. I find my teammates, and we deactivate our anti-grav belts. Excitement races through me.

We won!

Governor Jackson meets us when we land on the deck. His lips pressed thin, he hands Mick the ball-shaped trophy with miniature replicas of the Twelve Stations circling the top.

"Congratulations, Canoples," Governor Jackson says. "Don't set your hearts on keeping that trophy. We'll take it back next year."

I pull off my helmet and shake my sweat-soaked hair. His mouth falls open.

"Hey, gov," I say. "Long time no see."

He stomps away before I have a chance to ask if he brought Chuckles. Probably a good thing since I'm in too fantastic a mood for his drama. Beating his team is enough.

The team and I go to the lockers. After a sonic shower, we stow our gear and strut down the corridor.

"Promenade in an hour," Mick announces. "We're celebrating."

"We'll be there," I say.

Carl, Terry, and I take the long route. Cassie joins us near the other side of the stadium. I hold her hand while we walk. Before long, we reach the area near the SpaceDock. A klaxon clangs.

My buds and I halt in front of a porthole. The large, barge-like space ship slowing outside the porthole is what I expect. Fomalhaut has arrived.

"Did you tell your dad goodbye?" she asks.

"I won't see him," I say. "I can't after the way he acted at the trial and what he did to Mom."

No matter how hard I try, I can't forgive him. His adjudicator kept calling his criminal acts abnormal behavior brought on by an uncaring wife. The judge didn't believe the defense. More importantly, his willingness to blame Mom cleared up any lingering doubts I had about my decision on Jupiter.

"Forget about Dad," I mutter. "There's a party on the promenade soon."

Yet, we can't move until Fomalhaut leaves, until we make sure the pirates really are gone. A check of my surroundings assures me the station looks as good as ever. Maintenance has long since repaired the damage the pirates did. The promenade reopened a couple of weeks after the attack. We have access to Gut-Buster Pizza and an even better treat with a new food stand, Chili-Cheese Everything. It produces teen food covered with fiery hot chili and every kind of cheese in the galaxy. Carl, Terry, and I have already gone through everything on the menu, suggested a few other things, and are now working on a way to combine our fav pizza with their stuff.

The desire to own an upgraded Asteroids game vanished as soon as the arcades put in new equipment. We discovered Pirates and aced it within a month. Terry and Cassie are hard at work on a new version of Pirates, and they promised to share their earnings with Canoples Investigations.

"Will you ask for permission to visit your dad?" she asks.

"Nope." I sling an arm around her shoulders. She leans her head against me. "I don't want anything to do with him."

We can't see the loading process. No one can unless they work for Security. Luckily, Chief Pelham assigned Wade to patrol. He joins us as we wait for the ship to leave.

Fomalhaut jerks away from the loading tube. It hovers for a few seconds and then sails majestically away. In her bowels, Dad and his pirate gang will be going through the check in process. They'll never leave her. The judge gave them a life sentence.

"See ya. Never." I flip a hand in a sort of wave. "Come on, guys. We have a celebration to join."

Wade walks alongside us.

"Nice save at the end of the game," he says.

One other thing has changed. He no longer treats me like an idiot.

"Sure." I salute him. "Carl, Terry, and I took revenge for what Rendall did to you."

The year he graduated, Rendall not only humiliated Canoples, they partied here on the station to rub our noses in the defeat. That particular score burns every SpaceBall player on the station – fifty to two.

"Sure did." He returns the salute.

Now I know what it means to be an adult – his approval more than makes up for Fomalhaut's arrival interrupting our celebration.

"Time for a party," I say.

We run for the stairs. Some things will never change.

CHAPTER TWENTY-NINE

We run down the stairs and burst through the door on the promenade level. A sweet looking little girl hurtles toward me. Her arms circle my knees, and she hugs me hard. A pair of bright blue eyes glow at me, and I wonder just who this kid is. Behind the child, two adults smile in my direction.

"Thank you, BD," the man says. "If you hadn't checked on a locator beacon, my family would have died."

"I love you, BD." The little girl stares up at me.

I still can't place the kid, until a memory from the day that lasted forever returns. *Missy!* It's Missy and her parents, Bud and Cindy. Embarrassed heat makes me sweat all over my jumpsuit. Since that day, I forgot all about them. I'm sure my face looks like I solar-bathed at Mistlich when their filters broke.

"It was nothing," I say, and remember what Chief Pelham told me about his old friend. "Are you staying on Canoples now?"

"Sure are," Cindy says. "Bud will work with John in Security. No more Internal Security for my husband." She points toward the memory tree. "Go ahead and enjoy your celebration. You certainly earned it. That was an awesome game."

"Uh, great." My mind is too numb with the knowledge Missy will be around to attack me whenever we're close to come up with any other response.

Everyone turns toward the room when a huge roar rises from the crowd around the tree.

"Canoples Pirates are the best!"

My hands over my head while I pump my fists, I prance in front of my buds into the celebration. Blue and silver streamers surround the tables around the memory tree, with a sign announcing the winning team and their guests will sit there. We duck under the barricade and take over one of the tables. Chief Pelham and Mom sit across from me.

"We have a surprise for you," she says.

A cold shiver works along my muscles. She never punished me for breaking so many rules during the day that lasted forever. She wears a look indicating she is about to dump the ultimate punishment on me, one I dread. Images of red chips cascading on top of me and burying me alive intensify my fear. But I'm an adult.

"Uh. In case you forgot." I swallow hard.

Before I have a chance to land with both feet in scalding hot steam, the best smells in the world drift through the crowded promenade. Everyone stops talking as the owners of Gut-Buster and Chili-Cheese Everything walk toward us with what looks heaven on a table-sized platter.

The largest Gut-Buster in the galaxy has a brand new topping, covering all the others. Chili and cheese melts and steams around the meats and vegetables. The men groan as they lower the delightful treat in front of Carl, Terry, and me. We rub our hands together and reach for the first delectable slice.

Terry's PocketPad buzzes six times. He takes out the device and gulps. His horrified look as he stares at the screen makes me lean over the pizza to chow down on as much as I can as fast as possible. No case is more important than this food.

"Mom's on her way back!" he yells.

My hands poised over a slice, I look up. "That means–"

Alarm klaxons burst into life. Instead of the bulkheads slamming down, an opaque shield springs up in front of the reinforced tetra-flex. Fomalhaut streaks past, arcing around the station.

"Tell Fomalhaut's captain to dock at the cargo deck on Sub-Three," Chief Pelham says into his communicator and shoves past us. "We'll offload the prisoners into the holding area down there. Tell control to extend the station's shield around the ship as soon as it docks."

He, Wade, and Bud take off at a run. I look from my buds to the heavenly pizza. A once in a lifetime event is about to happen, and it's not the Gut-Buster.

"Io's erupting!" Cassie squeals.

She grabs my hand. With Carl and Terry flanking us, we dart through the mob and find a spot in front of the tetra-flex. Io is between Jupiter and us.

"How long before your mom lands?" I ask.

"They're already in the SpaceDock." Terry grins. "She said she'll find us after the eruption. So, you can't eat my Gut-Buster."

Will I eat my best bud's Gut-Buster while he has a reunion with his mom? Sure. No one likes a cold Gut-Buster, but this is different. No way will I miss an eruption I spent the last three years of school studying in different science classes.

"There it goes!" Carl says.

Silence falls over the promenade. I tighten my grip on Cassie's hand as a red-orange glow blossoms on Io. The glow grows larger and larger until I begin to think the station is in danger. But I dare not move until the show ends.

The glow expands until it encompasses Io and blocks our view of Jupiter. Everyone oohs and ahs as the volcano puts on a show all of us have anticipated for years. For just a mad second, I consider changing my mind about college, to attend the science institute near Mistlich, but I shake my head in denial. This looks good but no way do I want to spend the rest of my life grubbing around on planets and moons studying rocks and hoping I get to see another eruption.

After a while, we move away from the tetra-flex, to give someone else a front row spot. The four of us walk back toward the heavenly Gut-Buster, but the most horrifying sight in the world greets my eyes. Lisa and Jake gobble the last two pieces of the heavenly pizza and grin at us.

"They'll pay for that," Terry says. "No way can we let them get away with ripping off our pizza."

I try to pull away from Cassie, but an explosive roar comes from where Jake and Lisa stand. Both of them look around and flush bright red as they continue to spew gas everywhere. Then the most disgusting smell in the galaxy drifts around the promenade. Chief Pelham appears with Mom. Both wear gas masks, and I begin laughing as they take Lisa and Jake to the isolation room.

"They'll be stuck in isolation forever," Carl says. "But we still missed the best pizza in the galaxy."

"Or not." I point at Chili-Cheese Everything, where the owner carries containers over to Gut-Buster. "We just have to wait a little while longer."

My gang and I settle in our seats and watch Io erupting while waiting for the pizza. Wade and Chief Pelham walk up and straddle chairs a few minutes later.

"Sorry," the chief says. "I forgot about Lisa and Jake's appetites." He smiles. "Angela's in charge of their meals while they're in isolation. When I left, they were blubbering about surviving on vegetables and fruit."

I snicker. "Maybe they'll lose weight."

"I want pictures," Carl says. "They'll go perfectly with the ones of BD on the day he groveled."

The day that lasted forever left us with a lot of memories, but not all of them are good. The worst memory is of how my dad wasn't the man I always thought he was. That still bothers me during unguarded moments. The worst part? He's still on the station, but he'll leave as soon as Fomalhaut can sail through the ash cloud. I watch the eruption begin to wane and then check on the food.

"So, you're going to the academy at Mars," Chief Pelham says. "Given any thought to applying here for a position on Security?"

I keep an eye on the pizza now moving toward us. My stomach growls in anticipation.

"Yeah, but not for station security," I say. "I have a good thing going with C.I."

"You do." The chief nods. "Are you thinking private security?"

"Security consultant." I grab a couple of packs of the cure from Terry, no use taking a chance on ending up in isolation with Jake and Lisa until I get rid of all the gas this treat is sure to cause.

"Private security." Wade snorts. "I thought you grew up."

"I did." I face him. "And I read the news flashes, big bro. Twelve Stations is growing. The General Council approved another three dozen stations for manufacturing last week, to make room for the population increase."

Wow! I almost sound intelligent. I'd better watch it, or everyone will expect me to act more responsible.

"And?" Chief Pelham asks.

The men from Gut Buster and Chili Cheese Everything unload the second delectable treat in front of me. No one will stop me from eating my weight and more this time, not even the possibility of getting a case of gas. Just to be sure I'm not stuck in isolation with Jake and Lisa, I sprinkle the cure over several slices.

"They'll finish the ones around Canoples about the time I

graduate." I reach for a slice of the Deluxe Gut-Buster. "I figure you'll have enough trouble with all the people relocating to the station to work in them."

"We'll handle it," Wade says. "If a bunch of kids don't take up space at the academy looking for quick creds in private security."

"Yeah, but can you handle all the security issues with the manufacturing plants?" I ask. "Me and the guys figure we'll be security consultants to have one person for the owners of those new manufacturing stations so they'd don't have to bother Security about following the rules."

Carl and Terry chomp into their slices like a meteor shower hitting the station. I cup my piece in my hands, and I open my mouth to try out what I've wanted for weeks.

"That might work." Chief Pelham scratches his chin. "What will you do with C.I.?"

"I have two months to figure it out." I plant my elbows on the table. "Now. I'm behind and starving."

To the laughter of my big brother and the chief, I sink my teeth into the gooey goodness and try my best to catch up with Carl and Terry.

The End.

ABOUT THE AUTHOR

KC SPRAYBERRY began writing young, with a diary followed by an interest in English. Her first experience with publication came when she placed third in a Freedoms Foundation at Valley Forge contest while she was in the Air Force, but her dedication to writing came after she had her youngest child, now a teen getting ready to enter his senior year of high school. Her husband, son, and she live in Northwest Georgia where she now spends her days creating stories about life in the south, and far beyond. More than a dozen of her short stories have appeared in several magazines. Five anthologies feature other short stories, and her teen novel, *Softly Say Goodbye*, was released last year.

You can find her on:

Facebook:

https://www.facebook.com/pages/KC-Sprayberry/331150236901202

Twitter:

https://twitter.com/kcsowriter

Goodreads:

http://www.goodreads.com/author/show/5011219. K_C_Sprayberry

Blog:

http://outofcontrolcharacters.blogspot.com/

Google +:

https://plus.google.com/u/0/#115663651028837876590/posts

Pinterest:

http://pinterest.com/kcsprayberry/

Website:

http://www.kcsprayberry.com/

JacketFlap:

http://www.jacketflap.com/profile.asp?member=kathispray

Smashwords:

http://www.smashwords.com/view/profile/kcsprayberryffw

Made in the USA
San Bernardino, CA
14 September 2013